The Malan Witch

The Malan Witch

by
Catherine Cavendish

SILVER SHAMROCK

PUBLISHING

Dedication

To Colin, who made it all possible.

CHAPTER ONE

"Did you find the key, Robyn?"

"Not yet. Did you say third or fourth flowerpot?" Robyn clamped her phone more tightly to her ear. "Sorry? I can't hear you, Holly. The signal's really bad."

"...outbuilding...better..."

Robyn tasted salt as she battled the buffeting gale and kept close to the white painted cottage wall. The wind off the sea whipped through her hair, sea birds called overhead, and the waves broke over the shore five hundred feet below. Once she rounded the corner, away from the sea, it grew quieter. The outbuilding, which had once been the privy but now served as a wood store, stood a few feet away. A row of large flowerpots filled with some hardy geraniums leaned against the wall, their scarlet blooms defiantly clinging to their stems.

"Can you hear me now, Robyn?"

"Yes, that's much better. Thanks, Hol."

"You'll find you can only get decent phone reception there or in the kitchen. Everywhere else is a bit of a lottery. It's the same with the broadband and Wi-Fi, too. Some days it works like a dream and others... Fourth flowerpot, by the way."

"Sorry?"

"The key. It's under the fourth flowerpot. Got it?"

Robyn crouched down and moved the heavy pot. She retrieved the small fob containing three keys.

"One for the front door, one for the back, and I am guessing the old-fashioned iron one is for the outbuilding?"

"That's right. There's plenty of wood if there should be a sudden cold snap."

Robyn straightened up. An opportunistic blast of wind whipped around the corner and almost knocked her off balance. She sheltered under the eaves. "Is it always this windy?"

Her sister laughed down the phone. "I can't tell. I'm in London remember. It's bucketing down with rain here. But you're right on the coast on top of a ruddy great cliff, what do you expect?"

Robyn looked around, taking in the raw, majestic scenery of granite cliffs, grassland, and white-capped Atlantic Ocean waves. Gulls soared way above her head. "It's magnificent."

"You'd better get inside and unpack."

"You're right."

"Have a lovely time. Don't lose touch now."

"I won't. Lose touch, I mean. And yes, I fully intend to have a relaxing time. Resting, walking, reading, recharging my batteries." She didn't mention grieving. She didn't have to. *That* wouldn't blow away, even in this wind.

Robyn ended her call and dragged her suitcase the few feet to the back door. She unlocked it and stepped over the threshold of Malan

Cottage for the first time. As she did so, a sudden draft of stale air from within caught her off-guard.

Holly and Will haven't been here for a few weeks. That's all. The cottage needs airing.

Robyn shut the heavy door behind her which cut off almost all sound of the wind and waves. She took in the kitchen, replete with modern light oak fitted units that blended in with the three hundred-year-old stone-built home. It was certainly well insulated. Judging by the broad windowsills, the walls must be three feet thick at least. Above the front door, a transom window let in extra light, and, a small crystal vase lay on its deeply recessed ledge—a homely touch that was so typical of Holly. Sunshine coming through there would bounce off it, maybe creating multi-colored prisms of light.

Holly and Will had renovated the downstairs thoroughly a year ago when they first bought the ruined building to use as a holiday home—the perfect getaway from their busy lives in London.

Robyn moved through the kitchen and out into the living room. They had knocked down a wall, turning two rooms into one here, exposed the original stone and replaced what couldn't be repaired. Within the restored, recessed fireplace, a classic-looking wood-burning stove looked inviting. Maybe she would light that later. Robyn shivered and wrinkled her nose. What was that odor? Not strong but...it didn't belong here. This cottage should be sweet smelling. She made a mental note to invest in some room fresheners when she ventured into the nearby village of St. Oswell tomorrow.

She glanced out of the window. The view took her breath away. Grassland led to the cliff edge and out across the sea. White clouds were giving way to a perfect azure sky. Kittiwakes and cormorants—or were they shags?—executed perfect sky dances, gliding on thermals and swooping down out of sight. She could spend the whole summer sitting at this window watching their antics. Already she felt lighter, her spirits lifted. Who wouldn't, surrounded by all this beauty?

Her suitcase stood, almost accusingly, at the foot of the new wooden staircase. Robyn sighed. She dragged it upstairs, wishing she had packed lighter. Five closed doors awaited her. She started on the left and peered inside where she found a newly fitted bathroom, complete with bath, shower, and toilet. Next door revealed a separate toilet and handbasin. Handy for a family of four. The rest were bedrooms. One for Holly and Will and one each for the two children. Judging by the preponderance of pink with added unicorns, the first was Petra's, her nine-year-old niece. Next door, posters of dinosaurs proclaimed it to be seven-year-old Xander's room.

Deciding not to explore her inner child, Robyn opted for her sister and brother-in-law's room, where a perfectly white bedspread lay over a comfortable looking double bed. Two sets of windows gave majestic views of the ocean and the cliff walk. Typical of Holly, the wardrobe contained a plentiful supply of empty hangers, so Robyn quickly hung up her clothes and put her underwear in one of the many empty drawers. She glanced back at the bed and sighed. Why, oh why, did her sister choose white? Robyn was sure she would get a mark on it before the day was out.

She hoisted her empty suitcase on top of the wardrobe and paid a visit to the bathroom.

Upstairs contrasted quite sharply with downstairs. Here, the renovation had not been quite as drastic. The bedrooms were still mostly plastered. In the bathroom, some of the old wattle and daub from the original fifteenth-century timber-framed building had miraculously survived. Before she went back downstairs, Robyn investigated a small patch which had been preserved behind glass. Extraordinary how something consisting mainly of mud, clay, sand, animal dung and straw could withstand the test of time and extreme weather and still be in evidence today.

A sound of clattering from downstairs made Robyn jump. It sounded as if something had fallen onto the stone tiles in the kitchen.

She skipped down the stairs and hurried through the living room, that strange odor once again assailing her nostrils. It seemed stronger this time.

Robyn scanned the kitchen, searching for anything that could have fallen, rolled, or in some way made that noise. She moved closer to the far corner, next to the back door, bent down and picked up a large, flat pebble with a perfectly round hole in it. Robyn turned it over in her hand, noting how cold it felt. Almost freezing. Her fingers tingled when she touched it. The stone was completely smooth, maybe from spending thousands of years being tossed and turned by the sea. And that hole. Had someone carved it out centuries ago? There were no marks to indicate the use of any tool. Where had it come from? The door was closed, as were all the windows.

Puzzled, Robyn placed it carefully on the windowsill. She shrugged and decided on a mug of strong tea. She would have to take it without milk until she got to the shops tomorrow. A ten mile round trip to St. Oswell, on top of all the other driving today, didn't appeal to her. It was already after five and the shop might well be closing, anyway. As for a meal, Holly had said there was a pizza in the freezer. Robyn checked. Sure enough, thanks to her sister's impeccable forward planning, she had not only one but three to choose from. Robyn decided the spicy beef variety would fit the bill.

The kettle boiled and Robyn made black tea which she took into the living room. She shivered at the drop in temperature and decided to light the fire which was already laid. Before long, her toes were toasting nicely in front of a blaze scented with applewood. She leaned back on the comfortable settee and let her mind drift, hearing only the crackle of the flames.

The past year had been cruel. Her beloved Simon's diagnosis…the aggressive, inoperable brain tumor. The radiotherapy that could only ever be palliative, months of caring for him, quitting her job to be with him twenty-four hours a day. On top of all that, she had had to swallow the bitter pill of having to watch him shrink before her eyes. The Macmillan cancer nurses came daily toward the end, offering kindness and support when she most needed it, but even they could not stave off the inevitable final couple of weeks in the hospice. There, she stayed by his side, grateful for the dignified way he was treated. At the end he didn't know who she was, only that he needed to hold her hand. He cried if she had to leave him to go to the bathroom and always smiled when she returned.

Tears flowed freely down Robyn's cheeks now, as she recalled his passing, quietly and with dignity. He simply stopped breathing and was gone. Six months had passed since that day.

She couldn't cry when it happened. Not even at his funeral. A part of her still expected him to come home and open the door, wiping away the past months with one kiss. Her dreams would be filled with him, laughing, and even once, renewing their wedding vows as they had planned to do. She had woken from that one and turned to the empty space next to her where Simon should be sleeping. Even that hadn't brought on the tears she knew she needed to shed. That took another couple of weeks and came without warning.

She and Holly had gone out for a quiet drink in her sister's local pub. Robyn bought a round, set the glasses down and then... She couldn't stop sobbing. Holly drove her home, helped her inside, and stayed with her all that night. The next morning after a phone call to Will, her sister suggested Malan Cottage.

"You can rest there. Give yourself time to heal. Enjoy nature and get back on track, with nothing and no one to pressure you into doing anything you're not ready to do. Will and I are taking the kids to Croatia this summer, so you'll be doing us a favor by keeping an eye on the cottage when all the tourists are around."

Her sister had carried the lie off well. Robyn knew there was no planned holiday in Croatia. At least not until *after* Holly had promised the cottage to Robyn. Will was a good sort, and she had always got on well with her brother-in-law. He was good for Holly. He helped her let her hair down a little and be more spontaneous. And she had certainly done him proud this time. How could Robyn refuse? Hell, she didn't *want* to refuse. The sight of the same four walls day in and day out was becoming too much. Yet she knew going back to work was out of the question at the moment. Her doctor had said so. She was a high school teacher for Heaven's sake. There could be no question of sudden emotional breakdowns in front of a group of thirteen-year-olds.

The school said she could come back and had kept her position open, using substitute teachers to provide cover. She told them to fill it permanently with another candidate. It simply wasn't fair to her students, or to the school, to keep stringing them along when she wasn't even sure when—or if—she would be ready to return to work.

Robyn dried her eyes and drained the last of her tea. She must stop dwelling on the past. She stood and wandered over to the bookshelf, tilting her head to read the titles on the spines. Light crime novels by Kerry Greenwood and Joanne Fluke rubbed shoulders with James Patterson and Martina Cole. She certainly wouldn't be stuck for something to read this summer. Joe Hill's *NOS4A2* attracted her attention. She had been meaning to read him ever since that book came out, but hadn't found the time. Now she could. Removing it from the shelf, she flicked through the first couple of pages. Yes, bedtime reading sorted out.

Further along, she came to some much older volumes. Marcus Penworthy's *Demons of Cornwall*, and *Cornish Witches and Spells* by Robert Trethowan. She removed Penworthy and flicked to the content page, her eyes alighting on a short chapter headed *The Malan Witches*.

Robyn skimmed the first couple of paragraphs, learning that a local legend surrounded the fate of two women, Jowanet and Zenobie, in late Tudor England. Their surnames had been lost somewhere along the way, but they were frequently known by the word "malan," representing one of the Devil's right-hand demons. The same name as the cottage and the cove at the bottom of the cliff.

Robyn's phone bleeped. Someone had sent her a message. She replaced the book on the shelf and picked up her phone. Nothing registered.

She took her phone into the kitchen, and, the signal grew stronger. Still no message though. She flicked through a handful of emails before discarding them. Junk mail. Maybe she had misinterpreted the notification. At any rate, the first pangs of hunger were growling in her stomach. She switched on the electric oven and took the pizza from the freezer. Half an hour later, she was sitting at the kitchen table, munching away and staring out to sea.

The wind had died down and she decided on an evening walk, grabbing walking boots and a waterproof jacket. Outside, a pleasant sea breeze ruffled her hair, and the sun bathed her face in its warm glow.

Robyn set out, keeping well away from the cliff edge, reveling in the lonely calls of the gulls, the distinctive cry of the kittiwake, and the rushing sound of the waves breaking over the shore. Some distance ahead, she could make out two figures clad in black. They were standing still, and, she got the impression they were watching her. Hardly surprising. After all, the tourists weren't yet out in force, and, this was such an isolated area. Any newcomer would be bound to create even a smidgeon of interest.

She carried on walking, maintaining a steady rhythm, her feet swishing through patches of long, damp grass. Out at sea, the waves formed white horses, racing for the shore. In the far distance, she could make out the sleek lines of an enormous cruise ship, sailing its passengers across the Atlantic. It was too far away to make out if it was one of the giants. *The World* perhaps? Robyn shielded her eyes against the sun which was making her eyes water.

Sunglasses. She mustn't forget them next time she came out in the sunshine.

The ship gradually slipped away over the horizon, and, Robyn remembered the two figures that appeared to have been watching her. But they had gone.

She was out for a little over an hour as the sun sank lower, painting the sky a fiery red and reflecting on the waves until they too took on a kind of electric vermilion hue.

Time to return to Malan Cottage.

Thinking of the name reminded her of the book she had found. Malan. A devil, in the Cornish language. Why would anyone christen their home Devil Cottage? It hadn't been Holly and Will's choice. They probably hadn't a clue what it meant, unless they happened to have read that book. Robyn remembered their excitement when Holly told her they had bought the ruined building.

"It's going to take a hell of a lot of work," she had told Robyn over the phone. "But a year from now, it's going to be absolutely beautiful. Such a relief to get out of London for long weekends and holidays. And you can stay there too. Anytime you like."

It had been a bargain, of course. Lying there, derelict, an eyesore on a stretch of beautiful coastline. The property was owned by the Crown as the family who had once owned it had died out generations earlier.

Malan Cottage. How long had it held that name?

When she arrived back, Robyn circumnavigated the cottage looking for a plaque with a name on it. She found none. The house had simply acquired the name for some reason. Or maybe there had been a nameplate at one time and the builders had removed it.

Out of the corner of her eye, Robyn caught a movement by the outbuilding. A large black crow flapped its wings, cawing raucously as it flew off. Robyn unlocked the door and went inside.

The smell of applewood cloaked the previously acrid odor, and, the cottage felt warm and welcoming. Robyn stepped into the kitchen, and, her foot caught on something. She bent down and picked up a pebble. At first, she thought it was the same one as earlier, until she saw *that* one lying where she had placed it, on the windowsill. This too was granite, smooth and freezing cold, and, it had a perfectly circular hole off center. At least this time she had an explanation for its presence. She must have kicked it in with her boot.

Robyn laid it carefully next to its partner. The two were identical. Like twins. And there was something strangely comforting about them. Something that made her want to touch them. She picked them both up together, one in each hand. All her ten fingers tingled as if freezing cold. She hurriedly replaced them on the windowsill and stepped back, half expecting them to move.

Crazy woman. Robyn remonstrated with herself and removed her jacket, then hung it up on a coat rack adjacent to the door. She unlaced her boots and placed them underneath before padding into the living room where the fire had burned down to a warm, red glow. A glass of red wine would calm her rattled equilibrium. Sure enough, Holly had that covered too. In the kitchen, Robyn found a corkscrew and opened a bottle of Saint-Émilion she extracted from the small wine rack. She poured a generous quantity into a large wine glass and raised a toast to the sunset, a smile on her face for the first time in months.

Back in the living room, she picked up *NOS4A2* and within minutes was hooked—then seriously spooked. Sipping her wine, she read page after page, only pausing for a bathroom visit and to switch on lamps as the natural light faded. The fire burned down and went cold, but the room retained the heat at a comfortable level. Robyn continued to read well into the night until finally her eyelids drooped. She could no longer force herself to stay awake. By then she was almost halfway through the novel, but bed beckoned. She forced herself to close it.

Up in the bedroom, Robyn paused at the window. At home she wouldn't hesitate. She always slept with the curtains closed. No exceptions. But tonight, looking out over the sea, with the pale moonlight shimmering and reflecting off the water, she couldn't think of shutting them. Robyn let the fabric drop from her fingers and busied herself changing into a nightshirt. In the bathroom, she brushed her teeth and smiled at her reflection. A healthy glow she owed either to her earlier walk or the effects of the red wine tinged her cheeks, replacing her previously pallid, city complexion.

Feeling content for the first time in months, she climbed into bed and switched off the lamp, falling asleep within seconds.

Something woke her. Robyn sat up in bed, the room illuminated by the first signs of dawn. Shadows shrouded every corner.

One moved.

She cried out, grabbed the duvet tighter around her and stared. The shadow moved again. Yesterday's book flashed into her mind. Could her imagination be playing tricks on her? No, the shadow *had* moved. It really had. She hardly dared breathe.

A loud "*caw*" outside her window made her jump. The shadow fluttered and was gone. Robyn leaped out of bed. She checked the corner. Nothing there. It must have been the shadow of the crow. Maybe caused by the sun behind it? She gauged the angle. It hardly seemed likely as the sun was in entirely the opposite direction, but that must be it, mustn't it?

Robyn made a mental resolve to steer clear of Joe Hill's novel right before bedtime. In the future her late-night reading would consist of the lighthearted frolics and adventures of Kerry Greenwood's 1920s private eye, Miss Fisher. Her irreverent sleuthing was far less likely to induce scary leaps of imagination.

She glanced at her watch. It read five minutes before six. She could go back to bed but felt wide awake, so she might as well shower, have breakfast, and go for a walk. Judging by the early sunlight already glinting off the sea, it was shaping up to be a lovely day.

No matter which direction she turned, not a soul could be seen. Robyn welcomed the solitude. It matched her mood and calmed her frayed nerves. The farther she got from the cottage, the more absurd her fears about the shadows became.

Her hair blew into her face, threatening to knock her sunglasses awry. Robyn reached into the pocket of her jacket for a scrunchy she knew would be there. She scraped her hair back and secured it, then tucked the resultant ponytail into her jacket. She usually loved the feel of the wind in her hair but today's breeze seemed to come from all directions at once, blowing it into her eyes and mouth. Annoying.

The clearer visibility meant she could see much farther than yesterday; right up the meandering coastline and down the precipitous cliff to the deserted golden sands beneath. A kittiwake soared upward and released its distinctive "Kiiiii wahk wahk" cry. Her mind drifted back to her ten-year-old self, poring over an illustrated book of sea birds of the United Kingdom, where she had learned that the call of the kittiwake was supposed to be what gave the bird its unusual name, but as she watched the small gull swoop and soar, Robyn was reminded of her childhood thoughts. They had such cute little faces. If a cat was ever to be a bird, it would be a kittiwake.

She pushed her sunglasses a little higher on her nose and carried on with her walk. She had reached the same point as yesterday and had been out for half an hour or so. It was now after eight, and, the shops in the village would open around nine. The sun warmed her, and, her cares seemed to have faded, at least for now. This was doing her good. She would carry on a little farther.

A seagull landed in front of her, startling her momentarily, and she caught a movement out of the corner of her eyes. She focused on it. There, in exactly the same place as yesterday, stood two figures. No. Only one figure. The wind had caused her eyes to tear up yesterday, so maybe she had seen double then, but today, she was sure there was only one. Someone dressed from head to toe in black stood some distance away, staring over at her.

Without hesitation, Robyn began to walk toward her. It had to be a woman. The floor-length dress… A woman dressed out of time, or a modern-day Goth? The closer Robyn got to her, the more the figure seemed to fade and dissolve.

Robyn stopped, removed her glasses and squinted at her. It was impossible but the woman, if that was what she was, faded slowly and then blinked out altogether. How could that happen? How could a solid human simply disappear right before her eyes?

Unless she was never there in the first place.

Robyn quickened her step until she was running, covering the ground in under a minute. She touched a rusted barbed wire fence, joined to rotten wooden poles that looked as though a puff of wind could knock them over. Could one of these poles have created the illusion of it being a figure? Robyn doubted it. For all the enveloping clothing, the figure had been woman-shaped, not short and narrow like the piece of wood in the ground.

There was something else too, half hidden in the long, damp grass. Careful not to catch herself on the wire, Robyn pushed her hand through and tried to grasp it. Her fingers found wood. She wiggled it, and it gave slightly so she could raise it a few inches, enough to see that she was holding a blackened and charred plank of wood with an ancient rusty nail hammered into one end of it.

Curiosity getting the better of her, Robyn pushed at one of the supporting poles which gave way and fell to the ground, dragging down the barbed wire as it fell. She stepped over into the field and used both hands to tug at the resistant piece of timber. It gave a loud, sucking sound as if determined not to be released from its slumbering position. A few more tugs and it came away in her hands. Scorch marks covered its surface, but Robyn noticed the other end of the wood also contained a hammered-in nail. From somewhere deep in the recesses of her memory, a picture flashed in her mind of a sixteenth century engraving showing heretics nailed to crosses while flames licked their feet. There could be any one of a hundred reasons for this particular plank to have a nail at each end. Right now, that was the only one she could come up with.

Her mouth dry, Robyn gently laid the timber back down in its resting place.

She stepped back over the wire and replaced the pole as best she could. Her heart hammered as she made her way back to the cottage and she hadn't a clue why.

A little after nine-thirty, she parked her Hyundai i10 in the center of High Street. It was Tuesday, but the village seemed almost asleep. St. Oswell wasn't a place you drove through on the way to somewhere else. You had to want to be *there*.

Looking up and down the short thoroughfare, and, seeing the dozen or so cars parked there, Robyn wondered how anyone made a living. St. Oswell certainly seemed to have found itself stuck in a time warp. The small number of shops were all painted a uniform dazzling white, built of stone and clearly a few hundred years old. Trescothick's Butcher's Shop, a hairdresser, general stores, a pharmacy, a small medical center, a dentist, florist, a pub, café, and a clothing shop adorned both sides of the street. The church stood at the far end of the village. No sign of a bank, but an ATM machine had been fixed outside the general store—apparently the one concession to the march of technology this place had to offer. Robyn made her way there first and withdrew sufficient cash for today's grocery shopping before making her way into the general store where she proceeded to fill a small trolley with enough food and drink for the next few days. In the fifteen minutes or so that she spent in there, she counted six other people, and two of them were staff.

She paid for her goods and emerged into brilliant sunshine. The trunk of the Hyundai struggled with the load. With a little pushing and shoving, Robyn managed to close the tailgate. Feeling thirsty, she eyed Hedra's Tea Rooms, next door to the general store. A glass of something long and cold would fit the bill right now. She locked the car and made her way in.

An old-fashioned bell tinkled as she entered. The café was deserted. It had been some time since she had been in an authentic thirties-style tea room with a preponderance of chintz, from the gingham tablecloths to the matching curtains and polished dark wooden chairs with matching detachable cushions. She had begun to wonder whether the place was even open when a rustle sounded from behind the counter. A smiling, middle-aged woman, wearing a pristine white frilled apron, greeted her.

"Hello. Table for one, is it?"

Robyn returned the smile and nodded. "Yes, please. I'm parched. Do you have lemonade?"

"We do, indeed. I made a batch only yesterday evening. It should be nicely chilled by now."

Freshly made lemonade. She really had gone back in time. "That sounds lovely. Thank you."

The woman indicated a table by the window. "Is this all right for you?"

"Thank you. That's fine."

"You can sit and watch the world go by there."

Robyn resisted the temptation to say that it appeared the world had already gone by, and merely smiled.

"I'll fetch your lemonade. Would you like anything to eat? We have homemade lemon drizzle cake today."

Robyn felt her taste buds watering. "Just a small slice please."

The woman left her, and Robyn gazed out of the window. A solitary tabby cat crossed the road, nonchalantly, with all the time in the world and not the least wary of any traffic that might at any moment come rushing through.

That's because she knows there won't be any. Mine is probably the only unfamiliar vehicle she'll see all day.

"Here you are then." The waitress sat down a tall glass of cloudy lemonade and a substantial slice of delicious looking cake.

"Thank you. That looks great."

The woman hesitated, as if her curiosity was about to get the better of her. It did. "I hope you don't mind me asking but are you just visiting St. Oswell?"

"I'm staying nearby for a couple of months."

"Oh, where's that then?"

Robyn had, at that moment, taken a bite of the delicious, tangy cake. The woman waited patiently for her to swallow.

"Malan Cottage."

The woman's smile disappeared as if it had never existed, only to return a moment later but without the sincerity of its former incarnation. "Oh, Malan Cottage. That's…there have been cottages on that site since before any of these in St. Oswell."

"My sister and her husband bought it. They've done it up beautifully. I expect you remember it before."

The woman nodded slowly. "Oh yes, I remember Malan Cottage all right. In a terrible state, it was. Of course, no one would buy it, you see. On account of the legends."

"Legends?" Robyn took another mouthful of cake. She would definitely skip lunch after this sweet indulgence.

"Do you mind if I sit?" The woman pulled the chair back before Robyn could answer.

"Go ahead."

"I'm Hedra, by the way."

"Hedra? As in…"

"Hedra's Tea Rooms is mine. Hedra Trescothick is my name. There have been Trescothicks in St. Oswell since medieval times, maybe longer."

"I'm Robyn Crowe. I noticed the butcher's shop across the street."

"My father and my brother."

"Between you three, you keep St. Oswell fed and watered then?"

Hedra smiled and nodded. "You could say that. I suppose we do really."

"You mentioned legends? Concerning Malan Cottage?"

"Yes indeed. It starts with the name. Malan is connected with the Devil, one of his army you might say. All that area is informally known around here as Malan. When I was a girl, my mother always warned me to stay away from there. She said the witches would get me."

"Well, the cliff edge is really steep. She probably didn't want you falling over it."

"I don't think that was it. The cliffs are steep all round and she let me play everywhere else. No, there were two witches living there back in Tudor times, and they were burned for practicing the craft. That and being heretics. They denied the church and openly worshiped the Devil."

The image of that plank of wood flashed into Robyn's mind.

Hedra leaned forward. "You've gone ever so pale. Are you feeling all right?"

"I'm fine. Really. Do you happen to know where they were burned?"

"At the crossroads. You can't see it properly these days. Not far from your place, four cart tracks met, and they burned them there. They didn't have a proper trial. It was a lynching, really. They nailed the sisters to the crosses and set fire to a huge pyre they built at their feet. It was said their agonized cries and curses went on for hours.

Impossible, of course. It wouldn't take hours." She hesitated. "Perhaps best not to talk about that. Too gruesome."

"What did they do with the bodies...afterwards?"

Hedra shrugged. "Buried them, I suppose. There's a story that when the smoke cleared and the flames died down, there weren't nothing to bury anyhow. Their bodies were taken away by the birds. A huge flock of crows was seen circling their heads at one point. Then, quick as a flash, off they flew, and, folks said they took the spirits of the witches with them to Hell."

"Quite a story."

"Oh, there's more than that. The witches lived in the dwelling, and it came to be known as Malan Cottage on account of their activities. After they died, people reported seeing lights, flocks of crows, shadows dancing, all kinds of weird stuff... Are you sure you're all right?"

"What? Oh...yes." At the mention of the shadows, a sudden chill had raised goosebumps on her arms, but she needed to know more. After all, this was the place her sister had chosen for their second home. "Please continue. This is...fascinating."

"Well, it all came to a head when the burnings began."

"Burnings?"

Hedra nodded. "Farmers lost their crops when a sudden fire wiped them out one night. Barns were burned down with the animals still in them. Of course, the authorities, such as they were in those days, tried to blame some young boys, but the locals knew the truth. The witches were burned to death and seemed hellbent on taking their revenge by fire. They had to be stopped."

Robyn jumped as the door opened with a merry tinkle and a tall man with a blood-streaked apron poked his head around. He nodded at her. "Heat us up a pasty, will you, Hedra, and bring it over when it's ready?"

"I'll do it dreckly. I'm talking to this customer at the minute. She's staying at Malan Cottage."

His eyes grew wider. "Is she now, by Jove? Well, make it a little sooner than dreckly then, will you? I'm starving." He withdrew his head and closed the door behind him.

Hedra pointed at the door with her thumb, "That's my brother, Steven. I'm sure he thinks I was put on this earth merely to wait on him."

"If you need to get that pasty on—"

Hedra made a dismissive gesture. "He can wait a few minutes. Won't do him any harm. He could do with losing a few pounds, anyway." She laughed. "Now, where was I? Oh yes, the local people got together and decided they would have to fight using every tool they could against the witches, but these two were so powerful and so feared, no one would dare go up against them until one woman— Chesten Denzel her name was—volunteered. She knew the old magic, what some would call white magic these days. Her daughter went with her one night, but Chesten wouldn't let her go any further than the old fence which used to run right around the property. Her daughter pleaded with her, but Chesten refused. Finally, the older woman got her way and entered the cottage alone, and, her daughter saw the door slam shut behind her.

"She said her mother had prepared two poppets, one for each of the sisters. She carried silver bodkins which she would press into the dolls right where their hearts would be. The poppets themselves were dressed in fabric torn from the witches' shawls; ones they had been wearing over their dresses before they were hoisted up onto their crosses and burned. Chesten said this would make the magic even more powerful. She told everyone she would utter powerful incantations and spells and then secrete one doll in a hiding place by the door and one by the chimney, thus sealing up the two ways a witch could enter—or, in their case, re-enter—the cottage.

"But there's another entrance—the back door. What about that?"

"The back door wasn't there in those days. Malan Cottage fell down and was rebuilt three hundred years ago. I believe the builders at the time did find the poppets but, wisely, put them back in the same position in the new house. Evidently, it's worked because they haven't returned."

"And what about the windows?"

"To be on the safe side, she also took a chisel with her to carve witches' marks at each of the windows. By doing all this, the cottage would be protected."

"I haven't seen any marks. I doubt that they are there anymore with all the rebuilding that's happened"

"You need to do something about that. To be on the safe side, rub saltwater around each window in the cottage. Salt is anathema to witches. But I haven't told you the end of the story yet. Chesten managed to wrench the door open with great difficulty and called to her daughter that she had accomplished her mission. She stepped onto the ground outside the house. That's when a flock of crows or ravens appeared from nowhere and attacked her so viciously, they pecked her to death. Her daughter could get nowhere near to save her. Their task completed, the birds flew away, leaving poor Chesten Denzel dead on the ground. But the burnings stopped and gradually life returned to normal, leaving the legends to be passed on from generation to generation."

"With a little embellishment added to each telling, I should imagine." Robyn took a large swig of deliciously cold lemonade.

"No doubt about it."

"But this word, Malan, the cove is called Malan Cove. Did they practice their witchcraft there too?"

"Not that I'm aware. As I said, over the years, the whole area became known as Malan although you'll never see that on any map. Your sister's cottage acquired the name simply by association. I can't imagine any subsequent owner would ever have chosen it. Certainly not if they came from around here, at any rate."

The doorbell tinkled again, and, this time Steven Trescothick wore an impatient frown as he entered. "Hedra? Any sign of that pasty?"

"All right. All right. I said I'd be there dreckly."

"I know you and your 'drecklys.' Next week more like, if I don't keep on at you." He winked at Robyn.

She smiled back, thinking he'd be quite an attractive man if he smiled more.

Hedra pushed her chair back and stood. "Sorry, Robyn. Duty calls."

"No, not at all. Let me pay you. I need to get on, anyway." Not that she had any particular plans for today. Merely walking, reading, and generally relaxing.

Steven held the door open for her, and Robyn thanked him.

"Keep away from those witches now," he said.

"Enjoy your pasty," she replied.

Back home, she unpacked her shopping and put everything away. That done, she grabbed a pack of cooking salt and poured warm water into the washing-up bowl. She poured liberal quantities of salt into the bowl and watched it dissolve. Then, she hoisted it out of the sink and went around the house, using a kitchen cloth to wipe the solution around every window. Finally, she made herself a cup of coffee and stared out at the sea while she drank it. She thought back over her conversation with Hedra. Something bothered her. Then, with a sudden pang, she remembered. Hedra had said the builders three hundred years ago had replaced the poppets—the figures made to represent the witches—back in the same position in the new house. Hedra had remarked on how fortuitous that was.

Robyn closed the fridge and hurried out through the living room, into the short hallway. She peered carefully at the walls by the door, looking for any sign of something she might have missed. But this part of the cottage had been fully renovated recently. If Holly's builders had found anything and put it back, it must be covered with the new stone and plaster.

She went over to the fireplace. Was this even in the same place as it had been before Holly and Will bought the place? Then Robyn remembered. Holly had told her they had taken photographs of the cottage before and after. They had even made an album. One glance at the bookshelf and Robyn saw a dark blue leather-bound album, larger than the other books. She took it down and laid it on the table in front of the window. This was it.

Robyn flicked through the pages, noting the dilapidated state the cottage had been in. The chimney had collapsed into the living room, but it didn't take too much imagination to conclude that they had simply rebuilt it where it was. The front entrance, on the other hand… It was in the same place, but the original door had been hanging off its hinges and looked rotten in the photograph. There had been a timber doorframe and what looked suspiciously like wattle and daub, similar to that upstairs, but in a very poor state.

She turned to the next page and gasped. There was a picture of a worn, dirty and ragged doll with a large needle through its right side. Robyn read the caption in Holly's handwriting. 'Found stuffed doll near the door inside the wattle and daub wall. This went straight on the fire, and what a smell!'

Her heart beating faster, Robyn turned her attention to the fireplace. She stood flush with the—now cold—wood-burning stove and reached up, feeling around for any crevice where the other poppet might have been hidden. Her only reward for her efforts was blackened hands.

She hurriedly washed them in the kitchen and took her phone out of her pocket.

Holly answered on the third ring. "Hi Robyn, how's it going down there?"

"Hi… look, I need to ask you something. I've been looking at that album you made when you renovated the cottage."

"Looks a bit different now, doesn't it?"

"Yes, but I need to know, that doll you found near the front door."

"Oh, *that* horrible thing. Makes me shudder just remembering it."

"I'm sure. Did you really burn it?"

"Too damn right I did. Chucked it straight on the fire. It was the first time we used the wood-burning stove, actually."

"You said the doll gave off a smell."

"It was vile. I pulled the needle out of it and this stinking dark green ooze started dribbling out, so I immediately threw it in the fire and closed the doors. The flames shot up and turned this revolting shade of pea green. Then this awful smell started to fill the room. It was like a swampy, boggy stench mixed with a horrible sickly sweetness. I've never come across anything like it."

Robyn remembered the smell she had detected in the cottage when she first arrived. It didn't seem to be present now, but the way Holly described what she had experienced…yes, it could well be a much milder version. Robyn had purchased room fresheners today, so if it came back, she would be ready. But why was it there now after all these months?

"Robyn? You still there?"

"Yes." The line crackled, and Robyn moved around the kitchen. The crackling stopped. "Did you find another poppet?"

"Another what?"

"Poppet. Doll, like the one you burned. There are supposed to be two of them."

"Eh? Robyn, are you all right?"

"I'm fine. I've been into St. Oswell today, and got talking to this woman who owns the tea rooms. She told me about the legend of the witches who lived here in this cottage. They were burned to death for their alleged crimes, and, the locals were determined they should stay dead, so one of them made a doll effigy of each of them and stuck a needle through their heart. Then they buried one near the door and stuffed the other up the chimney. You obviously found the one by the door, but I can't find the one in the chimney, unless it's way up high."

"Then it would go up in flames wouldn't it?"

"Not if it was concealed in a crevice somewhere."

"Well, the chimney was pretty much destroyed as you'll have seen in the photograph, so I can't think where it could have been hidden. The builders never mentioned finding it, so I don't think it can be there anymore. Maybe a previous owner found it and got rid of it. Anyway, it's all superstition, isn't it? Pretty gruesome, if you ask me."

"Has anything...strange or odd happened to you when you've stayed here?"

The pause lasted a few seconds.

"Holly?"

"I'm still here. I don't know if you'd call it strange, but Petra had recurring nightmares the last time we were there. It was at half term and we stayed for four days, you remember."

"You didn't mention anything then."

"No, but I didn't think much of it. I still don't think it means anything. Not really. Just the imagination of a nine-year-old run riot in an old house. She woke up screaming three mornings out of four and always at exactly the same time."

"What time was that?"

"3:00 a.m. I went dashing into her room and found her shaking, telling me something had been in her room. Some horrible old hag by her description. She described her as dressed from head to foot in black and with horrible red eyes. I must admit, it sounded pretty scary. I think I would have been frightened if I'd dreamed that."

"And she's been fine since she got back to London?"

"Right as rain. She went straight back to her usual lively, noisy self. She had been a bit quiet and subdued on that holiday, but I put that down to the disturbed nights."

"And how about Xander?"

"No problems at all. Slept right through the commotion each night and thoroughly enjoyed himself down on the beach with Will, searching for baby crabs and stranded starfish. He's built up quite a shell collection as well. He'll show you when you come over next. He's been learning the names of all the creatures who formerly inhabited the shells. He keeps calling razor clams laser clams." Holly's light laugh tinkled down the phone.

Robyn smiled. Static crackled down the line. "Holly?" More static. "Holly, I've lost you." The phone went dead. "Damn."

The message tone pinged, and Robyn stared at the screen. Something flashed up, but was gone before she could read it. She clicked onto her message icon, but the last incoming call registered for the previous day, from her credit card company. Robyn clicked onto Holly's number and the phone rang out. Holly answered almost immediately.

"Hi, Rob—"

Raucous laughter chilled Robyn to the core. That wasn't her sister. She flung the phone onto the kitchen table. It skittered across the polished wood, coming to rest near the edge. She swallowed hard and retrieved it. "Holly, are you there?"

"What the hell happened?"

"Did you hear it? The laughter, I mean."

"No. All I heard was you calling my name, then a crash and the phone went dead again. I was about to phone you back when you came on."

"It's the bad reception, I suppose."

"Probably. Anyway, I'm going to go now. I have a dental appointment in half an hour. Mustn't be late."

"Chat soon. Have fun."

"Yeah…right. At least it's only a check-up."

Robyn ended the call and placed the phone back down on the table. Outside, a black crow landed on the roof of the outbuilding and blinked at her. It seemed to sense her thoughts.

But that wasn't possible, was it?

CHAPTER TWO

Jowanet and Zenobie Malan were two of the most despicable of women, Robyn read. *Born twins on a night when the moon waxed gibbous, their evil powers combined to make the people who dwelt amongst them terrified for their very souls. Their mother was the hag Erzabet who came not from the locality but from elsewhere, overseas. Their father was said to be the Devil's lieutenant, Malan, for no human male would set foot near her, such was her demeanor. When her daughters were of an age to fend for themselves, their mother disappeared, never to be seen again. From then on, the reign of terror began until, at last, the witches were caught, tried for their heinous crimes, and rightly burned. Naught remained of their bodies to be buried, for the crows took back what was theirs.*

Robyn closed Penworthy's *Demons of Cornwall* and replaced the musty-smelling volume back on the shelf. She moved restlessly around the room, tidying cushions that were already tidy, adjusting ornaments only to return them to their original positions, moments later. In the kitchen, she opened the back door and peered all around it. Maybe someone had reburied the second poppet somewhere there. After all, this was an entrance, even if it hadn't been in the witches' day. But there was no evidence of anything. As with the front entrance, if something was buried there, it was well and truly plastered in now. It could stay there too. Robyn doubted Holly would appreciate her drilling exploratory holes in her pristine walls.

She felt eyes on her and spotted the culprit. The crow had returned to its perch on the eaves of the outbuilding, watching her every move, its head cocked slightly to one side.

The day was turning chilly again and a real fire would be comforting. She could do with topping up the stock of logs in the living room. If only that bird would fly away. Robyn knew her fears were irrational, but she had the strongest impression that the crow was waiting for her to make a move and that when she did, it would swoop down on her like that flock had done to poor Chesten Denzel.

"Don't be so bloody ridiculous," she said out loud. "It's a fucking bird, for Heaven's sake."

Yes, good old *corvus*. Some of the most intelligent birds on the planet. That was another thing she had learned from her book of birds when she was a child. Some crows could be trained to perform tricks. All were quick learners and opportunists, especially carrion crows, and Robyn was fairly sure that was what was staring down at her now.

In a sudden impulse, she flapped her arms at it. "Go on, go away!"

The crow blinked at her, opened its beak, and emitted a loud *"caw"* before flapping its wings and taking off. It circled the outbuilding and flew so close to her, she felt the air stir and instinctively ducked back into the cottage. Another series of cries and it flew away.

The bloody thing's laughing at me.

Robyn grabbed the key from the hook by the back door and raced over to the outbuilding, where her fingers fumbled for the lock. It turned and she darted inside, slamming the door behind her. She flicked on the light switch, instantly illuminating the gloomy interior. The warm smell of the logs filled her nostrils while she collected as many as she could carry. It would be enough for tonight at least.

She looked around. Without the insulation of the cottage windows' double glazing, she could hear the seabirds calling. In the background, the waves breaking over the shore provided a comforting, powerful sound. The same sound the inhabitants of this place would have heard centuries before. The same sounds that would have punctuated the Malan witches' lives. Ultimately, these would be some of the last they would hear, too.

In addition to storing timber, the outbuilding had been used to winter a couple of animals, or so Holly had told her. Parts of it were the original structure, so there had been less of a need for renovation here as there had been in the cottage.

Some ancient and rusty farm implements stood propped against a nearby wall—a couple of vicious looking sickles and a few old cartwheels with spokes missing. A bridle, probably a couple of hundred years old and in a poor state of repair, hung on a nail. An array of garden tools in various states of disrepair and neglect looked as though they would fall apart if anyone tried to put them to use. Old bags that had contained sand and cement sat against one wall. All in all, this was a typical general dumping ground for things no one had use for anymore.

Robyn put her hand on the door handle and was about to turn it to leave.

"*Caw.*"

That bloody crow was back.

Robyn looked upward, hearing its claws as it hopped about on the roof. Her mouth ran dry and her palms sweated. As quietly as she could, she laid down the logs which had begun to weigh heavily. This was crazy. Holly would never believe it if she saw her sister now, cowering in an outbuilding, too afraid to come out because of a bloody bird. But there was something different about that crow. However much she told herself she was being fanciful, she couldn't shift that belief. She tried telling herself it was probably a different crow from the one that had taken such an interest in her earlier, but she didn't believe it. That was the same bird. For some reason, it had targeted her—although what for, she had no answer, except that it had something to do with that cottage and its dark history.

The seconds ticked by. Still she daren't move, daren't announce her presence. As if it mattered. She felt sure the bird knew she was there. All it had to do was wait.

Robyn eyed the sickle on the wall. She could use that to defend herself. That should do it. She tiptoed over to it and pulled it off the wall, surprised at how much it weighed. She turned it over in her hands, noting the rust, and the wooden handle, its surface pockmarked from woodworm. Nevertheless, it should do the job she needed it to do. The logs would have to stay where they were. Right now, her only priority was getting safely out of here and back in the cottage. Wielding the weapon above her head, Robyn threw open the door and stepped outside.

The crow cawed and swooped low in front of her, inches away from the flailing sickle. With her free hand, Robyn slammed the door shut. The last thing she wanted was for that bird to get inside the outbuilding.

It landed on the ground directly between her and the back door to the cottage. Robyn waved the sickle at it in what she hoped was a threatening manner. The bird stood its ground, head cocked on one side, beak slightly open.

"I will use this if you don't get out of my way." Did she sound convincing? Robyn's voice trembled too much, and the thought of actually attacking this crow…all the blood and… No. "Don't make me have to do this."

Still the bird stood its ground.

This couldn't be natural behavior. Surely this crow was intelligent enough to know she meant it actual physical harm. She was a threat to its survival, especially given she had a weapon. It made no sense for it to behave like this.

She brandished the sickle in both hands. "Go on. Fly away. Get out of here."

The bird moved slightly to one side and Robyn saw her chance.

She made a dash for it. The crow took off, wheeled around and came at her so fast, it scratched the back of her head before soaring upward. Robyn made it through the back door and slammed it shut before dropping the sickle. She put her hand to the back of her head. It smarted and she stared in disbelief at her reddened fingers. The bloody bird had attacked her. How badly, she couldn't tell. Robyn grabbed a clean tea towel and clamped it to her head before dashing upstairs to the bathroom.

Will's shaving mirror stood on the vanity unit, and she held it up behind her to see her reflection in the bathroom mirror on the medicine cabinet. She saw the cut, still seeping blood. She grabbed a washrag, wetting it under the cold tap before dabbing it against the wound and repeated this a few times before the cloth came back clear. In the reflection she saw the cut wasn't deep, but God alone knew what that crow's claws had been in before it attacked her.

She found a bottle of antiseptic and some cotton wool pads in the cabinet and braced herself as she applied the liquid to the wound. It stung so much her eyes watered, but she forced herself to keep dabbing until she was sure she had doused the wound thoroughly.

She returned downstairs and sat on the settee, trying to calm herself. But however much she tried to reason out what had happened, she couldn't escape one inevitable conclusion. That crow had deliberately attacked her. It had staked her out and meant her harm.

Her dreams that night were troubled. She kept seeing flocks of crows and, in between them all, a woman, ugly as sin, dressed all in black, muttering curses and pointing at her.

At 7:00 a.m., Robyn was up and dressed. She picked up Penworthy's book and resumed her reading.

The good people of the hamlet of St. Oswell were sorely troubled as one by one they fell victim to the most foul and sorry circumstances. Animals were burned alive, Master Trescothick's farmland laid waste by fire, and his firstborn son dead of a fever, and all within twenty-four hours. It was reported that witchcraft and sorcery lay behind the tragedies, and that the witches, Zenobie and Jowanet, known as Malan, were responsible from beyond their graves...

The account went on to describe how Chesten Denzel had been the only one brave enough to take on the dead sorceresses, and Penworthy gave, almost word for word, the same series of events as told to her by Hedra Trescothick. There could be little doubt that her family were one and the same with the Master Trescothick who had so tragically lost not only his farmland but also his son and heir.

Robyn debated whether to tell Holly what had happened. In the end, she couldn't stop herself.

She was met with an incredulous silence, followed by, "You were attacked by a...crow?"

Hearing the disbelief in her sister's voice made Robyn wish she had never mentioned it. In the background she could hear Will laughing, swiftly followed by a muffled shushing from Holly and the sound of a door closing.

Robyn took a ragged breath, still shaken from her bizarre experience. "I know it sounds crazy, and, I swear I didn't provoke it, but it deliberately went for me. I have the injury to prove it."

"Must be a rogue one. I have heard of them attacking, but... Have you been to the doctor? You might need a tetanus shot or some antibiotics or something."

"I'll be fine, Holl. Don't worry. I put antiseptic on it."

"I'm being serious, Robyn. You mustn't mess about with these things. If that bird broke the skin... well, you don't know where its claws have been."

"Okay, okay, to please you. I'll call in at the doctor's and make an appointment. I suppose I ought to register as a temporary patient as I'm going to be around for so long."

"As long as you do."

"I will. Honest."

They said their goodbyes and ended the call. Robyn picked up her car keys. She made sure the back door was locked before leaving through the front, checking first that the crow wasn't waiting for her and then mentally chiding herself for being so paranoid.

The medical practice, like everywhere else in St. Oswell, was quiet. After she had completed the necessary registration forms, she was told the doctor would see her straightaway.

He examined the wound and asked her what had happened. After Robyn explained, he sat back in his chair. "I suppose there is a hint of irony here, isn't there? Your name is Crowe and you were attacked by one. I shouldn't think many people could lay claim to that sort of coincidence."

Robyn pasted a smile on her face. "Probably not."

"The good news is the wound isn't deep, and it looks nice and clean. When did you last have a tetanus shot?"

Had she ever had one? Probably when she was a child. "I don't know."

"Best give you one to be on the safe side." He took a bunch of keys out of his pocket and disappeared out of the room for a few minutes, returning with a vial and a hypodermic in a sterile pack. "Where did the crow attack you?"

"Just outside Malan Cottage, where I'm staying."

The doctor froze in the middle of filling the syringe.

Was it her imagination or had his hand trembled? Only for an instant, but she was sure it had.

The doctor set down the empty vial. "And how are you finding things at...Malan Cottage?"

The jab was only the briefest of pin pricks. She rolled her sleeve back down while he broke the needle and shoved it into a bright yellow sharps box.

"It's a beautiful place. Such scenery. If it wasn't for that marauding crow it would be paradise."

He raised his eyebrows, mixing a look of surprise with one of almost disbelief. He recovered quickly. "Good, good. How long are you here for?"

"Probably the end of August."

"Well, my advice is to avoid that bird or maybe carry an umbrella, ready to jab at it if it comes near you. Crow attacks are rare, but they can do a fair bit of damage. They're big birds and they're built for tearing things apart. This one maybe has a nest nearby with young in it. That's the usual reason for such behavior."

Robyn didn't tell him she had gone way over the umbrella stakes, with a rusty but still deadly sickle, propped up beside the back door. She thanked him, and left noting that, although practice hours were still in force, no one was in the waiting room. *How does this village keep going?*

She toyed with the notion of calling in for another slice of Hedra's delicious lemon drizzle cake, or whatever was on offer today. Overhead, iron-gray clouds hung low, threatening a downpour. In the distance, a faint rumble of thunder punctuated a raven-colored sky. A faraway flash of lightning warned of much worse to follow. Robyn decided to get home before it hit.

The main road was barely wide enough for two vehicles to pass. The short drive up to the cottage was little more than a dirt track, likely to become sodden and muddy in heavy rain. The last thing she wanted was to get stuck in a mire. The lemon drizzle cake would have to wait for another day.

She made it back as the first giant drops of rain began to fall. Thunder crashed overhead, and a dazzling flash of lightning forked through the charcoal sky.

No sign of the crow, for which she thanked any deity who might be listening. Robyn closed the front door behind her as the heavens opened and the storm hit with a howling vengeance. Within seconds, rain lashed down so heavily she could barely see out of the windows. The eerie howling of the wind as it battered the cottage's sturdy walls, sounded like a pack of wolves defending their territory. Hearing it, Robyn felt like an unwelcome intruder.

She wrinkled her nose. That smell was back. Stronger this time.

Robyn opened a cupboard and took out one of the three room diffusers she had bought the previous day. She read the label. "Fresh Linen." She opened it and arranged its cluster of reeds into the jar. A pleasant, clean fragrance wafted upward. Robyn set it down on the kitchen windowsill and took out the other two. After fixing them up, she sat them at either end of the living room, Gradually, the sickly stench became overlaid with the homely scent.

The room grew darker and darker as the storm intensified. Crash after crash of thunder vibrated through the entire cottage. Forks of lightning flashed so bright they turned the gloom into brilliant daylight for a split second. Robyn switched on the lights in the living room and stared out the window at the back of the cottage. Yet more thunder shook the cottage.

Another searing flash of lightning lit up the roof of the outbuilding. Robyn gasped. In that briefest of glimpses, she swore she saw a huddled figure crouched there, as if ready to pounce. She looked again, peering through the murky gloom. There it was, too big to be a crow. As she watched, it spread out its black-cloaked arms. Another flash of lightning and it was gone.

For Heaven's sake, pull yourself together. Either it was the crow or maybe two of them close together, or you were imagining it. After all, the lightning flash had been so brief and what she had seen so indistinct. *The mind plays tricks...*

Eventually, the room grew lighter as the black cloud passed overhead, taking the thunder and lightning with it. The rain eased off. When she moved to the front, Robyn could see the forks of lightning striking the sea, while the cloud hovered overhead like some gigantic alien spacecraft.

A scratching noise behind her made her turn. It seemed to be coming from the chimney.

It's probably that bloody bird, come back for another go.

It stopped. She stood by the fireplace, in front of the wood-burning stove, for a couple of minutes but nothing more happened.

Robyn moved away and wandered into the kitchen. Feeling the first pangs of hunger, she set about making herself a cheese sandwich, with some of the crusty bread and local cheese she had bought yesterday. She settled herself at the kitchen table to eat it.

Looking out toward the outbuilding again while eating, this time with the sun once again shining and glinting off the rain-soaked stone, she saw at once the keys dangling out of the lock. She would have to retrieve those. Best do it now. She could bring the wood in too while she was at it. Robyn set aside the remains of her sandwich and made for the back door. Unlocking it, she glanced down at the sickle. She could hardly manage that as well as the logs. Besides, there was no sign of that bird.

She stepped outside and looked upward at the chimney stack, the roof of the cottage, and the outbuilding. The pungent smell of ozone filled the air. A few gulls soared overhead. Apart from that, the coast seemed clear. She made a dash for the outbuilding, opened the door, and grabbed as many logs as she could carry.

A couple of minutes later, her task accomplished, Robyn carried the logs with the intention of putting them into the nook by the fireplace. She didn't get there. At the entrance to the living room, she stared in horror at the sight that greeted her.

Soot littered the fireplace all around the stove, and something lay in the middle of it. Robyn prayed it wasn't a bird, especially not that crow. Whatever it was it didn't move. If it had ever been alive, it was either dead or unconscious now.

Robyn put the logs down by the door and retreated into the kitchen, her heart thumping wildly. She would need something to sweep up the soot and to dispose of whatever was lying there. Most importantly, she needed gloves as she had no desire to handle that…thing…with bare hands. She opened and shut cupboards until she found what she was looking for—a brand-new pair of yellow rubber gloves.

"Sorry, Holly. I'll replace them."

Armed with the vacuum cleaner—to which she had affixed the crevice tool— a small dustpan and brush, a rubbish bag, and wearing her sister's Marigold gloves, Robyn took a deep breath and returned to the living room. Her steps hesitant and her mouth dry, she approached the fireplace.

It soon became apparent that whatever laid in the soot wasn't, and never had been, a bird. When Robyn reached it, she poked at it with the brush before sweeping it into the dustpan. That was when she noticed the bodkin.

The second poppet. It had to be. Maybe the vibration of the thunder had dislodged it from its hiding place. Robyn set it to one side and vacuumed up the soot. The hearth would need a thorough washing, but the worst was over. Now she turned her attention back to the doll.

Gingerly, she touched it with her gloved hand. It was seriously charred as if it had been in a fire. She glanced back at the fireplace. Being up there for so many years was bound to have had some effect.

How the poppet had survived the collapse of the original chimney and the rebuilding, without detection, remained a mystery. Robyn certainly didn't see how she could get it back up there successfully. Of course, she could always conceal it somewhere else. By another entrance perhaps. The front door had lost its protection when Holly had burned its partner.

Robyn left the poppet in the dustpan while she went to investigate. The problem was the builders had done a good job of sealing up any nooks and crannies. Short of boring into the stone or digging up the floor, she was stymied. She looked down. Laminate flooring. Holly wouldn't appreciate a dirty great slice of it being removed, and who knew what was under that? Subfloor maybe, or more of the local stone?

She peered above the door. Perhaps the doll could be placed in its own little box above the door frame? Surely somewhere in the village sold trinket boxes.

Decision made, Robyn returned to the living room and stared at the dustpan. Empty. The poppet had fallen out. That's all it was. It had to be here somewhere. Maybe it had rolled under the stove... Rolled? It couldn't possibly do that. But she looked anyway, and poked her fingers as far underneath as she could.

She removed the filthy Marigolds and searched every inch of the room, coming up with nothing more than a few dust bunnies under the settee. Robyn washed the hearth and emptied the gray water down the sink. She swilled out the dustpan and brush, and returned the vacuum cleaner to its position in the small utility room off the kitchen.

All the while she worked, she pored over what could have happened to the doll, but however hard she tried, she came up with no answers. It had simply vanished.

And knowing that filled her with dread.

CHAPTER THREE

"That is some tale, Robyn." Hedra Trescothick sipped her tea as she shared a table with Robyn in the otherwise deserted café.

"I wondered if you had ever heard of anyone in that cottage having a similar experience. I mean, not just the doll thing, but also being attacked by crows."

Hedra took a large swig of tea. She seemed to be trying to decide whether or not she should tell her something.

"Please, Hedra, if you know anything, tell me. It's my sister's cottage, as I told you. They have two young children, and, their oldest had terrible nightmares when they were last there"

Hedra's eyes widened. "Boy or girl?"

"Girl. Her name's Petra and she's nine."

Hedra nodded slowly. "Yes, that would be about the right age."

"Right age for what?" Robyn felt like shaking the information out of her.

Hedra fingered her cup. "I expect you've heard of the Enfield Haunting? The two girls who experienced paranormal events? The youngest was eleven when she was apparently possessed by the spirit of an elderly and rather unpleasant man who had once lived in the house. They've made a lot of films about it."

"Yes. I've heard about that. It's also supposed to have been debunked. A lot of made up hokum."

"That depends on who you speak to. I don't think many around here would discount it so lightly. Not those of us who have history here."

"But what does this have to do with Malan Cottage?" Robyn couldn't keep the frustration out of her voice, and, it wasn't lost on Hedra, who frowned at her.

"It's the age, you see. The youngest girl was eleven years old. Your niece is nine, a couple of years or so away from puberty. That's when children—girls especially—are most susceptible to psychic forces. I've read a lot about it. In the case of Malan Cottage, it has happened too often to be coincidence. I'm guessing your niece's dreams involved witches. Or at least the popular notion of them. A woman, hideously ugly, dressed all in black, flaming eyes, that sort of thing?"

"Almost exactly that sort of thing, but how—"

"My mam told me. Back when she was a girl, she became friendly with a child her own age who lived at Malan Cottage. In fact, they were the last family to do so until your sister and her husband took it on. They didn't own it. They rented. Anyway, this girl, Elsie I think her name was, she started having nightmares where some terrifying character came after her. Then, she began seeing the same figure in broad daylight. Nearly sent her mad, it did. It got so bad the family moved out one night. Upped and left without a word to anyone. My mam never found out what happened to them, but she did tell me Elsie wasn't the first. It happened again and again down through the years whenever there was a young girl of around ten or eleven, twelve maybe, but rarely more than thirteen living there. The youngest I heard of was your niece's age. Sometimes the child would develop violent tendencies. There's one story of a girl trying to set her mother alight. The mother escaped harm, but they put the daughter in an asylum, where she remained for the rest of her life. She swore she could remember nothing of the incident, insisting a witch had made her do things she couldn't remember doing."

Robyn listened in mounting horror. If even a small proportion of what Hedra was saying had happened, it didn't bode well for Petra. The girl could be an insufferable little madam, but Robyn wouldn't wish any of this on her. Should she tell Holly? Would her sister even believe her? Ten to one Will wouldn't.

On the drive back home, Robyn changed her mind at least half a dozen times. She parked, and, after checking the skies and roofs, climbed out of the car and hurried into the cottage.

In the living room, her eyes were immediately drawn to the fireplace. There, lay the charred and filthy poppet. Without hesitation, Robyn darted over to it and picked it up, cringing at the unpleasant cramping sensation that shot up her arm.

"Where the hell have you been?" What was she doing talking to a disgusting doll with a rusty bodkin sticking out of it? Robyn took it into the kitchen and laid it next to the sink. Rummaging in the drawers, she discovered a roll of clear adhesive tape. She began tearing off lengthy strips. "Okay, this might not be very sixteenth century but it's the best I can do for now. You're not going anywhere."

Robyn grabbed a step stool from the utility room and set it up behind the front door. Holding the balancing rail with one hand, she carried the poppet with the other—the adhesive tape sticking firmly to it. She became aware of a faint, unpleasant, dank odor emanating from the foul thing. Once she had reached the top of three steps, she quickly positioned the poppet lengthwise on the ledge of the transom window and pressed down firmly on the adhesive tape. She then repositioned the glass vase to obscure it as best she could. With any luck, Holly might not notice it. She was a reasonable housekeeper, but not an obsessive one. In due course, Robyn would tell her what she had done—and why—but, for now, fingers crossed, the house was protected. Relief filled her.

Now there was no denying it. Her ability to accept the supernatural had changed. From being, at best, open-minded, the events that had occurred since she arrived at Malan Cottage had convinced her that the forces of darkness existed. More so, she was certain they existed in some form within this cottage, hidden, waiting for an opportunity to reassert themselves.

Robyn folded the step stool and stared up at the poppet's resting place. "You don't get to mess with my family," she said. "You'll have to come through me first, and I won't let you."

From somewhere nearby, a sigh drifted toward her. She looked around. No one there.

Back in the kitchen, her eyes were drawn to the two pebbles lying side by side on the window sill. On an impulse, she reached out and touched them, stroking the smooth surfaces. She found it strangely comforting.

For the next two days more rain lashed the windows as it swept in off the sea. A gale howled incessantly, sounding eerily wolverine at night.

On the second night of storms, Robyn laid in bed, unable to sleep. The noise of the wind had changed to an uncanny whistle, as it seemed to encircle the cottage. Unnerved by recent experiences, her senses were heightened. She fought the urge to pack her bags and drive back home. She had to see this thing through for the sake of her sister and her family. They had spent a small fortune on this place, and, Holly had confided in Robyn that the whole project had cost thousands more than they had originally budgeted for. There had to be a way of making this a safe home for them, and, Robyn was determined to find it.

As she lay propped up against her pillows, she formulated something approximating a plan. For the time being, she wouldn't tell Holly any more about what was going on, no matter what happened. That would only make her sister worry, and, she'd probably insist on coming down herself. There was no sense in both of them being here, dealing with this. Robyn needed to find out as much as she could about what she was dealing with here. For that, there could be only one person—Hedra.

Robyn resolved to go into St. Oswell the following morning and find out more. Maybe even enlist Hedra's help.

Finally, the latest storm blew over. By nine o'clock the next morning, fluffy white clouds sailed peacefully across a perfectly blue sky. The sea looked calm as a mill pond, the waves rolling in lazily and breaking over the sands.

St. Oswell itself benefitted from basking in the warm sunshine that reflected off the white-painted buildings. The improved weather had even brought out the locals. A few meandered up and down High Street.

Hedra had two customers when Robyn walked in. The café owner greeted her warmly. Robyn sat at what was fast becoming her usual table.

"It's Victoria sponge cake today, freshly made of course, with Corinne Tregowan's homemade raspberry jam."

"Sounds delicious. I'll have some, with a pot of tea today, I think. Thanks, Hedra. Could I possibly have a chat with you when you've got a minute? It's about the cottage."

Hedra seemed to have to force the smile onto her face at the mention of it. "Of course, I'll get your order now."

The couple at the next table over pushed their chairs back. Hedra took their money, wishing them goodbye and waving as they left. She disappeared out back and returned a few minutes later with a tray which she sat down in front of Robyn before proceeding to divest it of teapot, milk, sugar, tea plate, and a generous slice of fluffy sponge which oozed jam.

The tray now empty, she propped it up by the leg of the table and sat down opposite Robyn. "Now then, what can I do for you?"

Robyn brought her up to speed, watching the woman's face turn whiter and her eyes grow larger. When she finished, she noticed Hedra's hands were trembling slightly. "Are you all right?"

Hedra shook her head. "No, I don't really think I am. Your sister oughtn't to have burned that doll. Chesten Denzel died putting them in place. One for each witch. It had to be. One alone is not enough. One of the witches has been released."

"But surely, now that I have put the remaining poppet above the entrance, it won't be able to get in."

"What about the chimney? And you have a back door now."

"But that wasn't there when they were alive."

"What difference does that make? The house isn't the same as it was when they were alive, but it still needs protecting from them. When they were both where Chesten put them, the witches were imprisoned, locked in a void. Your sister changed all that. The one she allowed to escape will find the new entrance and get in."

"Then how can I stop that from happening?"

Hedra looked down at her hands, intertwining and unlacing her fingers. Finally, she said, "Have you found any other protection there? A mummified cat maybe? Or a child's shoe?"

"What? No, I don't think so. Holly hasn't mentioned anything. I could ask her."

"You should do so without delay. It was always the tradition to bury a dead cat in the walls to protect the house from witchcraft and other evil spirits. Same with a child's shoe. A child is innocent, you see. And shoes, being soft, mold to the foot, carrying the imprint of innocence—a powerful weapon against the Devil and his army."

Robyn fished her phone out of her bag. "I'll call her now."

Hedra nodded.

Holly answered quickly. She sounded flustered. "I have to go and pick Petra up from school. She's been sick and is complaining of a migraine."

"Oh, sorry, Holly. Just a quick call. I've been talking to a local lady about folklore. She was asking if you had found a mummified cat or a child's shoe buried in the cottage?"

"A mummified cat? Urgh, how gross. No. Nothing like that."

"No child's shoe either?"

"No... Good grief, what have you been talking about?"

"They're supposed to be...good luck charms, apparently. An old custom of the area."

"Well, we haven't found anything like that. We haven't done much to the outbuilding, but apart from that, I'm pretty certain we would have found anything in the house."

You didn't find the poppet up the chimney, though.

"Okay, I'll let you get off. Hope Petra's better soon. Bye."

"Your niece is ill?" Hedra asked.

"She's sick with a migraine. She gets them now and again."

"So, it's not a recent thing then? She didn't start having them since staying at the cottage?"

"Oh, no. She had her first one when she was about five, I think."

"We can be thankful for that then. Not thankful she gets migraines, but that the witch didn't curse her with them."

"Yes. Look, Hedra, would you come to the cottage? You know what to look for and, more importantly, where to look. I only found the poppet by chance, and that was because it got itself dislodged during a thunderstorm."

Hedra shook her head. "I'm sorry. I can't do that. I really can't."

"I wouldn't ask if I wasn't desperate to help my sister."

"It's not safe for me to enter that place. I can't do it. I'm sorry."

"But you wouldn't be alone. I've got my sickle. You should see it—"

Hedra stood up suddenly, her chair scraping the floor and nearly toppling over. "I can't go in there. *She* wouldn't like it."

"Who?"

"The Malan witch. Jowanet or Zenobie, whichever one of them is free. Chesten Denzel was my ancestor. We're directly related through my father's line. She was a Trescothick before she married. The Master Trescothick you read about, he was her father. That's why she was so hell-bent on revenge and wiping those witches out once and for all. Witches have long memories, Robyn. They can't go after *her* anymore. They've already done that. But they are quite capable of sniffing out any person related by blood. If I cross their threshold, I'm done for. I will have as good as signed my own death warrant." She burst into tears.

Shocked, Robyn leaped to her feet, and guided her back down onto her chair before grabbing a cup and saucer from behind the counter and pouring out a cup of strong tea. Hedra accepted it gratefully.

A few sips and she drew a ragged breath. "I'm so sorry, Robyn. I don't know what came over me. But I still can't come, much as I'd love to help."

"I quite understand. Don't think any more about it. But if you could advise me what I can do, I would be really grateful."

"You're going to have to be extremely careful, and, you will need to wear protection at all times. Witches can manifest as other life forms. It could well be the crow that attacked you is in fact one of the Malan witches. The fact that it seems to favor the roof of the outbuilding, and that it attacked you for going in there, may tell us something. It could be there is something in there it doesn't want you to find."

"You mean, like a mummified cat or a child's shoe?"

Hedra nodded. "Or it could be something else entirely. Do you have a rosary or a crucifix you could wear?"

Robyn shook her head. "I'm afraid we're not a particularly religious family."

Hedra thought for a moment, then reached behind her neck and drew out a piece of thin red cord. Suspended on it was a small flat pebble, with a circular hole off center, through which the cord was threaded.

Robyn gasped and pointed at it. "That stone. I have two just like it. What is it?"

Hedra's eyes opened wide. "It's a hag stone. You have two? Where did you get them?"

"One seemed to, sort of, appear one day. In the kitchen. The second one... I'm not sure, I think I kicked it in with my boot."

"I doubt that. It found you. My guess is they both did. Hag stones are powerful, and, if *they* find *you*, doubly more so. Someone is looking out for you, Robyn."

"But apart from you, I don't know anyone here."

"Just because you don't see them doesn't mean they're not there. Trust me. Those hag stones found you for a reason. You should thread them, as I have this one, and wear them always. Never remove them. Even when you have a bath or a shower, keep them on at all times. Do you have some red thread or cord?"

Robyn shook her head.

"I do. I'll fetch you some from my workbasket."

Hedra left her, and Robyn was alone with thoughts racing through her mind. Hag stones? She had never heard of them. And who had brought them to her?"

Hedra held a piece of red cord identical to her own and handed it to Robyn. "Make sure you attend to this when you get home. Don't delay."

"I promise. But can you tell me more about these stones? Where do they come from?"

"They are naturally forming. The hole is caused by the action of water eroding them over millennia. As they have been formed and molded by water, they retain its power. They are used by witches to aid the efficacy of their spells and cures. They can also be used to ward off evil. Beware of looking through the hole though. If you do, you will find it is a window—a porthole if you like—to the world beyond. The world of spirits. Beware of it. Don't be tempted to cross over. Now, tell me, did you notice if there was a horseshoe over either of the cottage doors, or in the outbuilding?"

Robyn closed her eyes, visualizing the entrances. "Not that I can recall."

"You'll need one for each entrance. There's a farrier about three miles up the road. He'll sell you some. Be careful to nail them up the right way though or your luck will, quite literally, run out. Hang it open end up. Best ask the farrier for used horseshoes, as they're more powerful."

"I thought they were just a good luck charm."

"Oh, they are, but they have stronger power in keeping witches at bay. Now, about that outbuilding. You've been in there. What did you see?"

"Not a great deal. It's mostly used for storing logs. There are some pretty ancient bits of farm equipment. A couple of bridles, sickles, that sort of thing."

"Were you able to look into the corners? Or see if there was anything stuffed into the walls, especially near the door?"

Robyn shook her head. "I didn't pay much attention, I'm afraid."

"Then I suggest you do as soon as possible. If I'm right, you may find something there which will help ward off the witch."

Hedra rummaged in her apron pocket and fished out her notepad. She wrote down a number and handed it to Robyn.

"Call me if you need any advice."

Robyn tucked it in her purse. "Thanks, but so far all I have is some personal protection. How am I going to get rid of the witch?"

Hedra stared at her. "I really don't think you can, Robyn. I think the best thing you can do is pack up, leave, and tell your sister to cut their losses and never go back to that cottage."

Robyn stared at her in horror. "I can't do that. I really can't. They've sunk their life savings into it. More, in fact."

"What's money when compared to the life of your children? Or indeed to the saving of their eternal souls?"

"But there has to be a way. Should I make another poppet and stick a darning needle into it?"

"It won't work. Not this time. It's far too late for that. Your sister saw to that when she burned the thing. I'm sorry, Robyn, but she made a fatal mistake that day. All you can do is limit the damage. Protect yourself. Get out of there, and, tell your sister to do the same."

Robyn arrived back home to find the cottage bathed in afternoon sunlight. Armed with her three slightly rusted horseshoes, a small bag of strong nails, and a hammer, she proceeded to hang the first one over the door of the outbuilding, taking care to check for the crow first. Confident it wasn't around, she hammered three nails in above the door, hung a horseshoe open end up, and then repeated the exercise over the front and back doors of the cottage.

She was coming around back to the front, when she noticed the window of the utility room partially open. "Damn." She could have sworn all the windows were closed. In fact, she couldn't remember opening any since her first encounter with the crow. Then, an awful thought hit her. When she had gone around the house, carefully wiping the windows with saltwater, she couldn't remember doing the one in the utility room. She had been in there, to collect the step stool to stand on while she wiped the transom window, but she couldn't actually recall wiping *that* one.

Robyn approached the utility room and peered inside. Something grabbed her attention and she recoiled in horror.

A single black feather lay on the floor.

Robyn grasped the hammer firmly and unlocked the front door, closing it firmly behind her. She stopped and listened. All seemed quiet and peaceful.

She made her way swiftly into the kitchen and through the open door into the utility room. Skirting the feather, she went up to the small casement window. She pulled it shut and noticed deep gouges in the hardwood frame. The handle wouldn't engage properly, and, she saw straightaway that it never would again. Something had forced this window open. It had taken considerable strength to do it, but, one thing became obvious, whatever had done it had used a sharp implement. Or maybe…a beak? The gouges looked remarkably like claw marks. Also, of all the windows in the cottage, this one wasn't a perfect fit. Holly had remarked on it, saying they would get around to having it fixed one day. Well, that day had well and truly arrived.

Robyn secured it as best she could, but one light tap, and it would open again. She went back into the kitchen, and searched, on her phone, for glaziers. Fortunately, there was one a few miles away. The call went to voicemail, but she had only just finished leaving a message when he called back. He couldn't do the job today, but would be out first thing in the morning. He did say he would call in on his way home and board the window up temporarily for her. Robyn knew she wouldn't get anyone to come out sooner, so she made the arrangement. At least, with the window secured, it would be safer than it was now. In the meantime, she would wash it with saltwater and hope for the best.

The two hag stones caught her eye. She picked them up, took out the cord from her pocket, and threaded them on to it before tying the resulting necklace around her neck. It reached down below her breasts. Too long. She almost cut it, but decided against it. No doubt Hedra had given her such a long cord for a reason. She would double-thread it instead.

The stones felt warm against her chest whereas they had felt ice-cold before she'd turned them into a necklace. A glow, a sense of increased strength streamed through her veins.

She returned to the utility room, forced herself to pick up the feather, and turned it over in her hand. If this was here, where was the rest of the bird?

CHAPTER FOUR

Robyn fell asleep almost immediately, and woke suddenly, with moonlight streaming through the window.

She lay listening, hardly daring to breathe, certain a noise had woken her. She touched the stone necklace and prayed the sound wasn't coming from the utility room. There was no wind tonight, and, the glazier had boarded the window up securely. She had rubbed saltwater into every possible inch of it. But what if it was all too late? What if something had already got in and was now trapped inside?

Robyn reached for the lamp and froze.

That smell. Wafting into the room. A mix of decay, mold, of smoke and marshes. A sickly-sweet undertone of death and rot. Next to her, something moved. As if someone had sat on the bed and was now watching her.

Robyn's mouth ran dry. Her skin prickled. Breathing in shallow gasps, she tried to will her hand to switch on the lamp, but she couldn't move. Her body wouldn't obey, as if whatever had entered the room had somehow paralyzed her.

The smell grew stronger, suffocating. Her eyes stung. Once again, she clutched at the hag stones around her neck.

The bed moved. Whatever had been there had stood up. The stench grew ever more powerful. Robyn felt the thing leaning over, almost touching her. She could feel its breath ruffle her hair.

Make it go away. Make it not be here.

Something touched her left shoulder. She screamed once, twice, again and again, but she couldn't drown out the laughter which started as a cackle then mounted to a screaming climax. It sounded like the crow, but more than that. It sounded like a crow-human. She clapped her hands to her ears. Nothing could drown out the hideous cacophony.

She cried out at the top of her lungs. "Go back to Hell, where you belong!"

It released her. She snapped on the lamp. The smell dissipated rapidly, and, she was once again alone in the room. But as she looked around, she spotted it, inches from her left shoulder. Another black feather.

Robyn scrambled out of bed and raced downstairs to the utility room. The window was still securely boarded up. She stood by the kitchen sink, panting, desperate to catch her breath. With the light off, she could make out the silhouette of the outbuilding. No sign of the crow there.

That's because it's in here.

Right now, fear gave her the strength and resolve to do what would have been unthinkable only a couple of days earlier. Maybe the hag stones helped. She had to find that bird—and kill it. She had the hammer and she had the sickle. Either of those would do the job, although a sharp kitchen blade might be a little easier to wield. Robyn rummaged in the cutlery drawer and found a large chef's knife. When she ran her finger along the blade, she was relieved to find it honed to perfection.

Now let that bird come anywhere near me. She gripped the knife tightly.

In the living room, the fireplace was free of soot, and a search behind chairs and the settee proved fruitless. She pulled out furniture and replaced it until she was satisfied nothing could be hiding there.

Upstairs, she searched all the rooms, ending with the one she was using. She found nothing. But it had been there, or something had. Something capable of leaving a solitary black feather. She had put the one she found earlier when she came home firmly in the kitchen waste bin. It couldn't have freed itself.

She ran downstairs and checked anyway. Sure enough, there it lay, on its own in the pedal bin. Robyn added the latest feather and let the lid fall.

From upstairs came the sound of something scurrying across the laminate floor, moving toward the stairs. Robyn crept out of the kitchen and stood at the doorway to the living room, which afforded her a clear view of the staircase. She moistened her lips. From her position she couldn't see the top of the stairs, but she could hear a light tapping sound, then another, getting nearer. She gripped the kitchen knife tighter, wishing her palms weren't sweating.

Another tap came, what sounded like claws jumping down from one stair to the next.

Then she heard another sound. A car engine, pulling up outside. Robyn retreated into the kitchen. Through the window she saw an unfamiliar blue car. The driver's door opened and Hedra emerged. Relief swept over Robyn. She wouldn't be alone now.

She opened the back door and almost dragged her new friend in. Hedra seemed unwilling at first, hanging back, pulling against Robyn, but then she sighed and crossed the threshold.

Hedra gazed anxiously around herself, as if searching for something she feared would be there to greet her. "In the end, I…I had…to come. I…couldn't leave you on your own with this…whatever it is…going on."

"You have no idea how relieved I am to see you, Hedra. It's all been kicking off here." Robyn brought her up to speed as fast as she could, keeping alert for any further sounds from the stairs.

"And it's up there now?"

Robyn nodded. "There have been two separate incidents and each time, it left a black feather. I'll show you." She fished the feathers out of the bin.

Hedra recoiled. "Please, put them back. I…I don't want to touch them. I'm surprised you can."

At that moment, Robyn felt the same. She dropped the feathers back into the bin and released the foot pedal to close the lid.

"At least you're prepared." Hedra indicated the hag stone necklace and the chef's knife Robyn had laid down next to the sink when she opened the back door. A sudden draught of foul-smelling air swept through the kitchen. Both women retched. "Dear God, whatever was that?"

"It happens from time to time." Robyn's eyes were watering, and she grabbed some kitchen roll, handing it to Hedra who accepted it gratefully. Robyn tore off some more. Both women masked their noses and mouths as best they could, holding the paper towels in place. It didn't do much to block out the stench, but it did muffle it a little, along with their voices.

"The only hope you have is to fight this black magic with white magic," Hedra said. "And I'm no white witch, but there is a wise woman in the village. I've spoken to her and told her what you told me. She said she would try to help you, but she is making no promises. Her family has also lived around here for generations, and she is only too well aware of the legends surrounding this place." Hedra retched and clamped the tissue close to her mouth, releasing it only to gasp.

"Please, can we get out of here? I'm going to be sick if I stay with this smell much longer."

She was already opening the back door. A welcome blast of fresh, salt-tinged sea air flooded the kitchen. Robyn followed her outside, nervously checking for any sign of the crow. She left the door wide open. It wouldn't be out here, would it? After all, she was as certain as she could be that it was still upstairs. Hiding in plain sight somehow. She must persuade Hedra to go up there with her. The two of them would have a far better chance of hunting it down and dispatching it.

"I saw that sickle," Hedra said, breathing deeply, as if trying to cleanse her body of the foulness inside. "With that and the knife, you've armed yourself well. Well enough that is, if your foe was human or a real bird. Neither is the case. I guarantee if you go back upstairs, the most you'll probably find is another black feather. The witch is taunting you. She knows she can scare you. She's playing with you until she gets what she wants."

"But I've done nothing to her."

"You hold the key to what she really wants, to free her sister from the remaining poppet."

"But that's in the house. I told you, it fell out of the chimney somehow. I couldn't see how I could put it back there securely, so I've attached it to the window ledge, above the front door."

"And as long as it remains there, she can't get to it, so she will torment you until you finally give in and take it down."

"But that isn't going to happen."

Hedra smiled. "You don't know her power. She will do anything and everything she can to get you to take that poppet down and destroy it by fire the way your sister destroyed hers. She doesn't merely have the power to shapeshift...turn into another creature...she can invade your dreams, possess your mind, force you to do her will. And you have already experienced her physical power. She can attack you at will and cause you actual harm. Maybe worse..."

"How do you know all this, Hedra?"

"I told you. I've been speaking to the wise woman. Her name's Meliora. Meliora Penrose." She grabbed Robyn's arm. "Robyn, please take the greatest care. I know you don't want to cause your sister great financial hardship, but this place is possessed by evil."

"I appreciate your help, Hedra. I would like to meet Meliora as soon as possible. Will she come here, or should I go to her?"

"I can ask her to come here. She doesn't have a phone or the internet or any modern gadgets because she believes they poison the atmosphere around her. She'll want you to unplug anything electrical and to switch off your phone at least half an hour before she arrives. And when I say everything, I mean it. Switch off all your electricity. If the weather's stormy and makes the room dark, only candles may be used."

"I had no idea witches were so sensitive to electricity."

"Not all of them are. Meliora is a little…different, shall we say. Eccentric, certainly. No one knows exactly how old she is, only that she is, by far, the oldest one in our community. There seems never to have been a time when she wasn't around, yet she never ages. Oh, when you see her, you won't believe me. She looks a hundred if she's a day. But what I mean is, she has always looked like that. I can remember her from when I was a girl, and she looked the same as she does now."

"She sounds fascinating."

"She is. But, Robyn, you must promise that you will do whatever she says. Even if it sounds bizarre. Everything she will do or say is for your own safety. Do you understand?"

"I do. How soon can she come?"

"Now. I can bring her here within the hour."

"Thank God," Robyn breathed. "I don't think I could have stood another night on my own with that thing roaming around."

Hedra gave her a strange look, not a smile exactly and not a frown. Robyn's cautious optimism took a tumble.

"What else? Is there something you've not told me?"

"If you truly can't bear the thought of another night in this cottage, with or without Meliora's help, you shouldn't stay here. I've warned you; she makes no promises. The magic may work. It may work straightaway, or it may take a while. There might be a need for her to return. Or it could fail miserably."

"I understand. No, I do. Really. But this is the best chance we have, right?"

Hedra nodded. "Right now, it's the only chance you have. Or else you might as well do your sister a favor, take a match to the place and burn it down."

"And claim on the insurance."

Hedra shook her head. "They would discover it was started deliberately and you would end up in court. Prison most likely. Their methods are very sophisticated these days."

"I wasn't making a serious suggestion."

"I'm glad to hear it." Hedra unlocked her car door. "You know, it's strange. In the village I never think of locking my car, but out here, I did it automatically. Stupid really since any threat around here is supernatural and has no regard for locks and keys." She nodded up at the horseshoe over the outbuilding door. "I see you did as I suggested."

"And there's one over the back and front doors to the cottage. Doesn't seem to have helped though."

"That's because the evil was already in the house. It went in through there." Hedra pointed to the boarded-up utility room window.

"I know, I feel so stupid, but I missed that window when I wiped all the others down with saltwater. I've done it now, of course, and someone's coming to fix the glass later today. Perhaps I'd better put him off until tomorrow, as Meliora is coming."

"Probably a good idea. The damage is already done, after all."

Robyn didn't like the finality in her tone. As Hedra drove off, Robyn rang the glazier and postponed him until the following day.

She stared at the open back door, not daring to return inside. Instead, she closed it, without locking the door, and looked toward the cliff. She could still taste traces of that awful smell. Some blasts of fresh sea air should help to cleanse her palate.

The sun warmed her cheeks and blew hair around her shoulders. She mustn't go far, but there was no need to re-enter the cottage until the white witch arrived. Except…

Damn. She had to go back in to switch the electricity off as Hedra had instructed her. She took a deep breath, turned back, and opened the back door.

This time, no smell greeted her beyond a faint aroma of fresh linen from the reed diffusers. The mains electrical panel was in a cupboard near the front door. She went to it and flicked the twin circuit breakers to the 'Off' position, cutting off the electrical supply to the entire cottage.

Without the usual faint whirring of the fridge and freezer that she normally didn't even notice, the cottage was eerily quiet. A sudden impulse to check all the upstairs rooms sent her up the staircase, looking around her as she ascended. She had to be sure she hadn't missed something, like a window, open a chink, that could ruin everything. After the utility room fiasco, she had to be *sure*.

At the top of the stairs she caught her breath. Another solitary black feather lay on the floor. Robyn skirted around it, gripping the knife tightly and raising it, ready to strike.

She poked her head round the door of her bedroom. All quiet

In Xander's room, everything was as it should be.

Then she went into the room next door.

A movement stopped her in her tracks. Over by the wardrobe, a hunched figure in black slowly straightened. As if in slow motion, it turned, one claw-like hand extended. In profile, Robyn had no idea whether she was facing an oversized crow or a small human. She held her breath and clutched the knife to her chest with both hands.

The creature kept on turning. It almost faced Robyn, and raised itself, lifting its claw-like feet off the ground, hovering a few inches in the air. It threw back its black hood and let out an earsplitting *caw*. Then, it drew its arms together in a broad, sweeping gesture. Instinctively, Robyn brought her hands up in front of her face as the witch's glare hit her full face. A quick glimpse of staring, red veined eyes, gray skin, pockmarked with short black quills, black lips and a worm-like black tongue. It flapped its arms like wings and rushed toward her.

Robyn fell onto her knees and cowered, as the thing brushed her hair, and its malevolence defiled her soul. Waves of utter blackness and despair flooded her mind. It vanished, taking its foulness with it. Robyn's heart thumped. This was Petra's room. The source of the child's nightmares became clear. The Malan witch threatened her too. Robyn prayed she wasn't already too late.

She made a resolution. Petra must never stay here again. Not even for one second did she want her niece to experience what she had, for her nightmares to become real. Whoever the witch had been when she was alive, there wasn't one shred of humanity remaining in her.

Robyn raced out of the room. She dashed downstairs, grabbed her coat and bag, along with her car keys and those to the outbuilding. The back door banged behind her. Up above, on the eaves, the crow watched her, its black eyes blinking, head cocked to one side.

"You evil bitch." Robyn spat out her hatred and realized, in her haste, she had left the knife behind.

The crow watched her, and Robyn sensed it was enjoying the sight. She unlocked her car door and climbed in, locking the doors behind her. She couldn't see the crow now. She would wait here until Hedra returned with Meliora. Time enough then to retrieve her knife.

A beating of wings. The crow landed with a thump on the hood of her car. Robyn pulled back in her seat. It hopped closer until its beak was less than an inch away from the windshield. Its eyes blinked at her as she stared, mesmerized at first. Its stare seemed to penetrate her brain. She had to get away from it. It seemed to be drawing her into itself. Sucking the lifeforce out of her. Trying to possess her and take control of her mind, her senses, maybe even her soul.

Robyn caught sight of the clock on the dashboard. Hedra had been gone three quarters of an hour. But that wasn't possible, was it? Surely, she had only been sitting in the car for a few moments. The crow was still there, still staring at her. And that fixed gaze was not the normal stare of a crow. Something hideous lay behind those eyes. However crazy and impossible it might seem, this creature surely had to be responsible for this inexplicable passage of time.

"What the hell have I ever done to you?" Robyn was shocked by the desperation in her own voice.

She shut her eyes and prayed. Prayed that Hedra would come and that Meliora would be able to rid her of this terrible curse. The waves crashed on the rocks beneath, and the crow issued its infernal, hideous *caw*.

In the distance, Robyn heard a car engine. Moving closer. She opened her eyes. The crow paused as the car drew up. Robyn suddenly remembered her phone and quickly switched it off. Hedra emerged and helped an elderly woman out of the passenger seat. The crow had switched its attention to them. Robyn waved at her visitors to get their attention, and the woman with long, streaming white hair looked straight at her. From this distance, it was impossible to gauge her age. She moved easily enough, no evidence of a walking stick. Her long, flowing maroon coat reached down to her ankles, and her feet appeared shod in old fashioned black button boots. With Hedra beside her, she advanced toward Robyn's car. The crow stopped its vile cawing and stood, motionless, studying her every move.

Meliora reached into the sleeve of her coat and extracted what, to Robyn's untrained eye, looked like a bent twig. The old woman murmured something, raised it, and pointed it directly at the crow. This time, her voice sounded loud and strong, so loud Robyn heard every word through the locked and shuttered car.

"Be gone, foul pest of the air."

The crow flapped its wings, gave a final, loud *caw*, and flew away.

Robyn unlocked the doors and staggered out of the car.

The old woman lowered her arm and replaced the twig up her sleeve.

Hedra introduced them. "Robyn, this is Meliora."

Robyn put her hand out, but the woman shied away from it.

"No, I may not touch you, girl. I am still infected from the journey in this contraption." She nodded at Hedra's car. "And you have the smell of someone who has touched something of power recently."

Robyn's confusion must have shown on her face. Hedra explained. "Meliora means you have touched something electrical, or maybe your phone in the last few minutes? I did say half an hour, at least, should elapse from when you killed the electricity, to Meliora's visit."

"I know. I'm sorry. I switched off the power soon after you left, but the phone was in my pocket and I only remembered it now. Something happened. I lost track of time... That crow..."

"So, you are infected, but the house is drained?" Meliora said.

"I...suppose so."

Hedra nodded. "That would be it, Meliora."

Meliora blinked startlingly, her eyes much brighter than Robyn had ever seen in a woman of her supposed antiquity. She found her continued gaze uncomfortable, invasive. In its way, almost as scary as the crow's. Once again, she felt some force—this time from Meliora—penetrating her brain, searching, prodding, uncovering anything she could find. What if she turned up something she didn't like? Would she refuse to help her?

The frightening surrealism of Robyn's day continued. Time seemed to stand still, out there, with the breeze ruffling her hair. Hedra stood stock still. Robyn felt sure this wasn't her first time with Meliora pursuing her craft. Into Robyn's mind, out of her control, flashed glimpses of the past year, forcing her to relive them.

Simon. Images of their past life at first. Happy, smiling, drinking champagne, walking along cliffs near Scarborough, their lips almost numb from the cold but still managing salty kisses as the rain whipped their hair.

The scene shifted. She held Simon's hand as they watched the sunset on their Nile cruise. The evening sun burned the sky in vivid reds and oranges, while the ship slid past the ever-changing movie-scape of the riverbanks and the gentlest of breezes tickled their skin.

Another scene shift. They sipped mojitos, their feet aching from clambering over fallen stones as they visited fabulous temples and soaked up the heady atmosphere of the ancient pharaohs. Simon's favorite had been majestic Abu Simbel while, for Robyn, it had to be the breathtaking temple of Karnak at Luxor toward the end of their unforgettable vacation. Happy, glorious memories she hadn't allowed herself to recall for so long, fearing the regret and sadness they would bring, but now, maybe Meliora was helping her in some way to come to terms with the impossible.

Then again, maybe not. All too soon, the happy images dissolved into a hospice room. An emaciated and confused Simon stared up at her with weary eyes. Before he had lost the ability to speak, he had gripped her hand. "Be happy, Robyn. Let me go and you live for both of us. Live a long and happy life. Promise me."

Robyn remembered bending and kissing him, wishing he didn't smell so much like the environment around them. Clinical. Sanitized. The nurses did a marvelous job making sure he was kept as comfortable and clean as possible so, inevitably, in this pristine clean ward, everything smelled the same. Linen, air, patient. She knew she should be grateful. As his condition deteriorated, they had their work cut out, but Simon always lay in clean sheets, even though every day, he seemed to shrink a little more.

Until the last day. Once again, her mind forced her to relive the agony of the last goodbye, of seeing his eyes close for the final time. Feeling his grip on her hand slacken. Hearing his final breath, so faint, like a bird or a kitten, barely enough for his body to exhale. The nurse's gentle touch on her arm and how Robyn had eventually moved away in a daze. Simon's spirit had left his body and now she would have to go on without him. The task seemed impossible. Six months on, it still seemed daunting, but she realized she had been making progress. One foot in front of the other.

Until this. What should have been a real tonic, a chance to rest and recharge her much depleted batteries had become a fight for survival.

Meliora raised her hand and made a curious clutching gesture, opening and closing her fingers like a half fist. She lowered her hand and, as she did so, the images faded from Robyn's mind, replaced with the sound of the waves and the birds soaring overhead.

Meliora nodded and touched Hedra lightly on her hand. "The girl is cleansed," she said, as if Robyn wasn't there. "We may proceed."

A waterfall of questions, some of them indignant, poured into Robyn's mind. She bit them all back. It wouldn't do to antagonize possibly the only chance she had to rid this cottage of the evil presence that had infested it.

Meliora looked around her. She pointed to the outbuilding door. "We begin there."

"The keys are in the kitchen," Robyn said.

"Please fetch them. We must not delay."

Robyn took a deep breath and half ran into the cottage, grabbed the keys, and raced out again. Meliora and Hedra waited as she fumbled with the lock before opening the door.

She stood back to let Meliora through, exchanging a look with Hedra, who put her finger to her lips. So that was the way of it, speak when you're spoken to, question nothing, and do what you're told. It went against her nature, but if that's what it took…

Meliora approached the back wall and peered upward and to the left and right. "Here. This is where we will find it. Help me please."

She started to scrabble at the array of farm tools and general detritus propped up against the wall. Robyn whispered to Hedra. "What are we looking for?"

Hedra shrugged and moved to join her friend. Robyn followed.

"We will know when we find it," Meliora said. "But I am certain there is something here. Something that will help us in our quest."

Robyn dragged away old, almost empty bags of sand, cement, and garden tools.

Meliora exclaimed, "It's here."

She held something in her hand. At first Robyn couldn't make it out. When she did, she backed away. "Oh my God, it's a dead cat."

"Don't be alarmed. Robyn," Hedra said. "This has been protecting this building. It has made it a hiding place, a place of sanctuary which you have reinforced with the horseshoe."

Robyn moved closer. The dead animal was completely desiccated but still recognizable. All four paws, jaw open, teeth intact. "And that protects this place?"

"None better," Meliora said. I shall put it back but now we know there is at least one place where the witch may not enter. As we go about our work, we may have need of that knowledge and of this sanctuary."

Robyn wondered if the cat had died of natural causes or been sacrificed. She decided, under these circumstances, it was better not to ask.

"We will leave the door unlocked," Meliora said.

Robyn and Hedra stood aside to let her pass, and she led the way outside. Meliora looked upward. Robyn followed suit. No sign of the crow

"You must invite me in," Meliora said to Robyn. "Or else I cannot enter."

"Please come in, Meliora," Robyn said. "And Hedra too, of course."

Hedra smiled. "It must seem strange to you, but we have to assume the witch is watching. If you don't invite Meliora inside your home, it will weaken her magic."

Robyn refrained from asking how.

Inside, the smell had returned. Robyn wrinkled her nose. "It's worse than ever."

Hedra put her hand to her nose, but Meliora didn't seem to notice the foul stench.

She stood in the center of the living room, extracted the twig from the sleeves of her robe, and raised both hands high. "Witch of Malan. Feel my presence. Feel the power of the elder tree. Tell me your name."

The silence felt like a heavy blanket, stifling. Robyn coughed. Between that and the stench, she found it difficult to breathe.

Seconds ticked by.

"I need salt," Meliora said.

Robyn raced into the kitchen and grabbed the cooking salt. She brought it to Meliora.

"Put it on the floor next to my feet and come and stand by us. We need its protection."

Robyn nodded and did as told. Meliora poured salt through her fingers, creating a circle and enclosing within it a familiar symbol. A five-pointed star. Images from late night horror films flashed through Robyn's mind.

"We stay in the center. Whatever happens," Meliora said. "And be prepared that a lot may happen. Don't believe anything you see or hear. Don't even trust anything you feel. Jowanet and Zenobie were both powerful witches. Perhaps among the most powerful ever. They were the daughters of Malan who takes his orders from Satan himself."

Hedra slipped her hand into Robyn's whether to offer or receive comfort, she didn't care.

The air grew darker, until it seemed night had descended hours early. Robyn couldn't even see the far end of the living room.

Meliora raised her hands again. The elder twig, or wand as Robyn knew it must be, quivered a little. "The witch is here," Meliora said.

Hedra and Robyn huddled closer together.

Meliora's voice rang out, strong, challenging. "Witch of Malan. Tell me your name."

A stench of open graves filled the room causing Hedra and Robyn to choke and retch. Scared of falling out of the pentagram, Robyn clutched Hedra tighter, anchoring her own feet slightly apart to increase her stability. Hedra did the same.

"Witch of Malan, I repeat. Tell me your name."

A voice, like a raucous whisper, surrounded them. "Jowanet, of this place."

"Did you hear that?" Robyn asked.

Hedra nodded, her lip quivering.

Meliora called out again. "Jowanet, daughter of Malan, of the Devil's brood, what do you want of this place?"

"My...sister." The voice uttered the word with a snake-like hiss. "My sister is bound and shall be free."

"Do you see her?"

"She is hidden to me. But I will find her."

"My love..."

Robyn jumped at the familiar voice. It couldn't be. "Simon?"

"Don't believe the witch," Meliora cried. "It lies. It will always lie."

Simon's voice called again, soft, seductive, so close and real. "Robyn. Come to me. Look, I'm here. Waiting for you..."

"Can you hear that?" Robyn asked Hedra. "It's Simon. He's here."

Hedra shook her head, her face white and her eyes huge.

Meliora laid her hand on Robyn's arm. "What you are hearing is not real. She wants you to step out of the circle. She wants to destroy us."

"Robyn? See? I'm here. Your Simon. I've come back."

A faint glow, a silvery mist taking form and gaining in strength, emerged from the shadows outside the pentagram.

"I see it too, Robyn," Meliora said. "But I see something hideous where you see something wonderful."

Robyn only half heard her. Simon stood before her. Her Simon, well and healthy. Alive, dressed in her favorite white shirt and black trousers. He held out his hand to her.

"Come to me. I'm here. We can be together. As we planned. We can live in Paris. Go back to Egypt. Anywhere you want, just come to me."

"Robyn! Robyn!" Meliora shook her arm, but Robyn ignored her. "You see someone you love, but I see the truth. A dwarf, a creature that has never drawn breath in this world or any other. An evil spirit sent by Jowanet, maybe even from Malan himself."

Her voice faded in Robyn's mind. All she could see, all she could hear, smell and feel, belonged to Simon. Healthy, vibrant Simon. The man she had loved since the day she met him was calling to her. The grief melted away. He stood inches away from her. Reaching out to her. Smiling in that familiar way. She was aware of Meliora shouting at her, but she could no longer process the woman's words.

"Simon?" she said. Meliora and Hedra held her back as she put her foot out. She tried to shake them off, her eyes focused on Simon, her head full of her love for him.

She became vaguely aware of a chant. Meliora at first, then Hedra joined in. To Robyn's horror, Simon was fading.

"No! Come back. No! Simon! Please! Take me with you." Robyn fought to pull herself free of the restraining arms. "Get *off* me, you bitches!"

The mist descended and he had gone. Meliora and Hedra supported her as she slumped, sobbing her heart out. "Why did you stop me? Why?"

Hedra stroked her forehead. "It wasn't real. None of it. I saw nothing. No one."

"I saw what was really there," Meliora said, her voice gentler than Robyn had heard it before. "You would not have loved what you went to. Trust me. That wasn't your beloved Simon. He is, I can assure you, at peace."

"How do you know?"

"Because I felt his spirit when I touched your mind. He watches over you, but not like that." She thrust her forefinger in the direction of where the vision had appeared.

"You must have loved him very much," Hedra said. "I'm so sorry."

"I did. I do. I… It was so real. And the emotions…"

"Jowanet has the power of her ancestry," Meliora said. "She can conjure up images, thoughts… Not much is beyond her. Remember what I said. Believe nothing. Stay firmly within the circle and let me do my work."

"I'm sorry, Meliora."

"It's to be expected. It's your first time."

"I don't plan on there being a second."

Meliora's lips turned up slightly at each corner. A smile? Probably not. She removed a small bottle from her coat pocket and sprinkled a few drops all around the edge of the circle enclosing the pentagram. A strange, but not unpleasant, smell wafted up and momentarily helped to cloak the persistent graveyard stench. An overtone of aniseed was about the only individual scent Robyn recognized.

"Tincture of agrimony, angelica, myrrh, mugwort, and anise, among others," Meliora said. "Powerful herbs to fight the witch."

A loud hiss sounded behind Robyn and moved around the circle, accompanied by a swirling gray mist.

"Hold tightly," Meliora said as the three women clung together. The wind blew stronger, threatening to tear them apart. Meliora's chants grew louder, like plainsong in a cathedral. They echoed as they somehow bounced off the mist. "Be gone from this place, Jowanet. Your sister is lost to you. She is lost to time. There is no room for you here. No purpose in your remaining. Get you gone. Back to Hell where you and your kind belong."

The mist swirled faster. Howling gave way to screams, then hollow cries.

"Souls in torment," Hedra called above the din.

"Don't trust it," Meliora said. "It has not finished with us yet."

As she said the last word, it stopped.

No wind, mist, or darkness. The room lightened and the women looked around. Everything looked clean and tidy; nothing to indicate the hurricane they had lived through. Even the salt circle and pentagram remained intact. Hedra and Meliora stood behind Robyn.

"So even that was simply an illusion," Robyn said.

No reply.

She glanced over her shoulder. No one there. She was entirely alone.

And then, she wished she was.

The hag towered above her. "Give her to me. Give me my sister."

Robyn shook her head. Terror grabbed at every nerve end, but she would not show fear. Somehow, she would work out what had happened, and she would get through it. "I don't have your sister, and, I don't know where she is. Except in Hell."

Jowanet's lips curled, revealing rotten, blackened tooth nubs. Her skin was covered in the same spiky quills Robyn had seen on the hag in Petra's room.

The witch spoke again. "Your sister released me, and now you will do the same for Zenobie."

"And if I do, will you leave us all in peace? Will you leave here and never return?"

Jowanet grimaced. "You seek to bargain with me?"

She was mocking her. Robyn's anger began to replace her fear. "You think I have something you want. Something you must have. Yes, I am bargaining with you. Perhaps." Meliora's warning not to believe anything she might hear or see came back to her. Simon hadn't been real. Perhaps this wasn't either. Maybe she was still in the circle and the witch was trying to tempt her out of it so she would reveal the poppet. "On second thoughts, Jowanet, I will not bargain with you. I choose not to."

Flames shot from the witch's eyes. But it was cold fire that hit Robyn and knocked her to the floor, winding her. A force dragged her back up on her feet. It pulled her out through the kitchen and tossed her outside, flinging her across the yard to the outbuilding where she collapsed against the door.

Sanctuary.

Maybe it was real and maybe not, but right now it presented the best hope for survival. Dazed and disoriented, Robyn forced herself to her feet, relieved that no bones seemed to be broken. She yanked the door of the outbuilding open and staggered inside.

The comforting smell of applewood greeted her. She sank to the floor, heedless of the grime and sawdust, grateful to lean against some old sacks. Exhaustion overwhelmed her and she fell asleep.

"Robyn! Robyn!"

She drifted back to consciousness to find Hedra shaking her.

"Oh, thank goodness. I thought she'd got you this time. For sure."

Robyn struggled to sit up, her back, legs, and arms protesting, feeling bruised after her earlier battering. "What happened? One minute I was inside the pentagram with you and the next you had both gone."

"No, Robyn. That's not what happened. Look again. Look around you."

Robyn blinked. Her eyes were smarting. She rubbed them, trying to focus. Images swam in front of her gaze. She should be in the outbuilding, but when she looked down, she saw laminate flooring. Her body ceased to hurt. The sacks she had been leaning against turned out to be Meliora. The three of them were still inside the pentagram.

"So, I never left?"

Hedra shook her head, as Meliora helped her up. "It was a close thing. She nearly had you. Another inch and you would have been out there, at her mercy."

"But I thought I was. She came at me, threw me…"

Meliora turned to face her. "She got to you through your mind and your grief. We have to get you out of here before she regains her strength. Not even your hag stones could protect you. You've been through enough today. More than enough. We can only be grateful that all her efforts seem to have sapped her energy too, but we do not know how long it will take before she is strong again."

"The outbuilding…it's sanctuary. You said so," Robyn said.

Meliora shook her head. "It is not enough for you. Not now that she has managed to get so close to you. If we remain here any longer today, I will never succeed. You will come with us now and stay with Hedra overnight. If we hurry, we can leave the pentagram without harm to ourselves. I will also place mugwort under the entrance mats for both the front and back doors. It will help to ward her off, although for how long, I cannot tell. She is the most powerful witch I have ever encountered, and I have met many over the years. Now, come, we cannot remain here. I can already feel her stirring."

Robyn shook her head, trying to clear her wits, and leaned heavily on Hedra as Meliora extracted two pouches from that seemingly bottomless pocket of hers. She touched one with her wand before placing it under the front door mat and then repeated the action with the back door.

"Take your keys," she said to Robyn. "We'll lock everything up. No sense in leaving the house open to burglars."

How incongruous to think of something so relatively harmless at this time. Robyn wished with every atom of her body that a house burglary was all they had to fear.

Hedra's cottage was small, old, and smelled pleasantly of fresh flowers, a large vase of which stood in the center of a highly polished oak dining table. They had dropped Meliora off at her home, and only then did Robyn switch her phone back on.

"Make yourself at home," Hedra said.

"I haven't brought any clothes, not even any underwear," Robyn said.

"Don't worry about that. If we'd hung around while you packed a case, we might not have made it out of there."

"And tomorrow we go back and do it all again."

"If you want to cleanse that cottage, it's the only option we have. I agree with Meliora. That witch is far more powerful than any I have ever heard of, even more so than the legends say. We need to rest and recover our strength. Exhausted people don't win wars, and that's what we're engaged in, make no mistake."

Robyn's phone rang. Her sister. She sounded out of breath.

"Robyn? Oh, thank God I've got you at last. I've left a ton of messages."

"Sorry, Holly. I had the phone off, and the reception's bad as you know and—"

"Never mind that. You're there now. I'm calling about Petra. I'm really worried about her. She's started having those nightmares *here*. The same ones that she had at the cottage. She keeps seeing a...well, a sort of witch, I suppose. She woke us all up screaming around three this morning swearing it was in her room. We checked, and, of course, there was no one, but we did find something lying on the floor. At first, I thought it was only a bit of rubbish and picked it up. But it wasn't. It was a long black feather. It looked like it had come from a crow."

Robyn nearly dropped the phone. "Oh my God."

Hedra stood by her elbow. "What is it?"

"Who's that?" Holly asked.

"A lady from the village. Hedra. She owns the café."

"Oh... yes... Robyn, I don't know what to do. How did that feather get in there? Petra swears blind she didn't bring it in. Xander said he's never seen it before, either. I believe them. You should have seen the shock on their faces. Neither of them is a convincing liar. Has anything been happening to you down there?"

Robyn put the phone on speaker so Hedra could listen in.

"You'll have to tell her," Hedra said.

"Tell me? Tell me what? *Robyn.*"

Robyn wished Hedra hadn't said anything. Now she would have to come clean. "Okay, there have been some...incidents. That doll you burned. It was an effigy of a dead witch, and by removing the pin and burning it, you released its spirit. It's called Jowanet, and it's come back. It's looking for the effigy of its twin sister so it can destroy it and free her. Then the two of them can resume their reign of terror. They were burned to death long ago and are hell-bent on revenge."

There was silence at the end of the phone and then Holly's voice, little more than a whisper, as if she couldn't bear to speak any louder. Or maybe she was afraid to. "You mean...you *believe* that stuff? My practical sister, and you believe in witchcraft now?"

"If you had been here, you would too. I've seen the witch who's scared Petra so much. She's been haunting the cottage. That's where she and her evil sister lived back in the sixteenth century."

"But that cottage wasn't built—"

"That doesn't matter. It was built on the same land, in the same place, even using some of the same stone. All the evil they built up stayed behind. As long as their poppets were hidden in the cottage, they were both trapped and couldn't escape, but—"

"Oh my God, it's all my fault."

Robyn heard the tremor in her voice and wished she could have spared her sister this, but there was no going back now.

"There's no point in blaming yourself. What's done is done, and, now we have to find a way of stopping it."

"That's like trying to put a champagne cork back in a bottle."

"You could say that, but we have to try. That's what I've been doing today, with a lot of help from Hedra and a local white witch named Meliora. We've had quite a battle, but we must go back tomorrow and try to finish the job. The missing poppet turned up, and I've put it somewhere it can hopefully do some good—"

"I'm coming down there."

"No, Holly, you mustn't. You must stay there with Will and Xander. You have to protect Petra. Don't let her out of your sight. The witch can shapeshift. That crow's feather you found? I told you I was attacked by a crow, and that was her. I've also found single black feathers here when I know she's been around."

"But it's my mess. I can't leave you to go through whatever you're going through because of my stupidity."

Hedra grabbed the phone. "Holly? You don't know me, but please listen. I have lived here all my life, and my family for generations before that. The Malan witches are part of our folklore. Jowanet is free, and she will stop at nothing to find her sister. She's now trying to use your daughter who is of the right age to be bent to her will. You must do as Robyn says. Stay away, keep Petra close, and whatever you do, make no attempt to come down here. Take your whole family and stay somewhere else for a few days. Whatever you do, make no attempt to contact your sister, not by phone, email, or text. Keep total silence."

Holly let out a deep breath like a whoosh down the phone line. "Okay. I'll call Will."

"Don't discuss where you' re going to stay until you see him in person. And don't tell Petra at all. Let it be a surprise when you get there, wherever it is. Don't mention anything about the place now, either."

"I'll get back to you as soon as I can, Hol, I promise," Robyn said.

"Be careful. You're the only sister I have, remember."

"You too. Love you all."

"Love you more."

The call ended and Robyn brushed away a tear.

"I'd switch that off, if I were you. Just in case."

Robyn weighed the phone in her hand and depressed the on/off switch. The screen went black, and the phone buzzed briefly as it shut down. Robyn tucked it back in her pocket. "What *are* we going to do now?" she asked.

Hedra shrugged. "I don't know, but Meliora will be busy preparing something, of that I'm sure. She won't give up even if this kills her. She'll keep fighting."

"A sunny day for dark work," Hedra said as she handed Robyn a mug of strong tea. "I remembered you like it almost black."

Robyn managed a smile as she spread marmalade on a hunk of brown toast. "We were brought up on strong tea. Mum couldn't abide weak, milky stuff."

"She's not with you anymore then?"

Robyn shook her head, feeling the familiar welling up of emptiness at the loss of the people she loved. "Mum passed away three years ago. Cancer. Dad died shortly after. He had an aneurysm, and it was very quick in the end. He was never the same after Mum died. Holly and I both felt it happened for the best, even though they were both so young. Only early sixties."

Hedra sighed. "My Phil passed ten years ago from a heart attack, and, there still isn't a day goes by I don't wish him back with me. It hurts, doesn't it? Mind you, it's worth the hurt for all the good times we had. We didn't have any children. I couldn't, you see. Medical stuff. You don't have any either, do you?"

Robyn shook her head. "It wasn't something Simon and I ever thought about. We were happy as we were. I don't think I would have made a particularly good mother, anyway. Now that he's passed away, I wonder if it was the right decision." She looked down at her mug, tears pricking her eyes.

"Right," Hedra said. "Let's get these things washed up and then we'll drive over to Meliora's. Your phone is still switched off, isn't it?"

"Yes. It's in my bag." Robyn picked up her plate and mug, and followed Hedra into the tiny kitchen, where she picked up a tea towel and dried the breakfast things, after Hedra washed them.

"Have you ever done this before? Assisted Meliora on a house cleansing?" Robyn asked.

"Not as such. I've seen her in action a few times. People tend to call on her when they move to a new house. She comes along with a sage brush and bells, cleansing each room of any negative energy. When Phil and I moved from our previous cottage to here, she did the same for us. It really made a difference. You could feel the atmosphere lighten in every room. Amazing really."

"And do you keep any charms here? Mummified cats or anything?"

Hedra gave a light laugh. "No cats, but we did find a child's shoe buried under the hearth when we had the gas fireplace installed. We reburied it, and Meliora came and provided a blessing."

"I wonder what she's planning for today."

"I really don't know. It will have to be something pretty powerful though." Hedra emptied the sink and dried her hands, before untying her apron and hanging it behind the door. "Right. It's just gone ten. Time to pick up Meliora. Ready?"

"As I'll ever be."

Meliora looked tired and paler than she had yesterday. She carried a wicker basket containing a selection of bottles and clusters of herbs, at least one of which stank.

"Asafetida. We will burn this to cleanse the home. And I've brought fumitory, also to burn. Horehound seeds will protect us, hopefully better than the salt did yesterday, but I shall use the two together. The rue is an extra protection. We are well armed against evil spirits today, and, I have my spells and a few other items. I shall need you to be brave, Robyn. You must do exactly as I say at all times and without question. Is that understood?"

"Yes, Meliora."

Hedra piped up from behind the wheel. "The witch has found Robyn's niece up in London."

"I feared as much. Is she harmed?"

"No. Just frightened. I have told them to leave their home and stay somewhere else for a few days. There is to be no communication between Robyn and Holly in case Jowanet should latch onto it."

"She's a wily one, make no mistake about it." A loud sigh seemed to emanate from deep within the old woman's soul.

Robyn turned to look at her. "Are you all right?"

Meliora touched her hand, and Robyn couldn't hide her surprise at the iciness of her fingers. "Age has crept into my bones today, child. That's all. Nothing for you to worry about." She withdrew her hand and clasped both together in her lap. "Now, we must plan. We will base ourselves in the outbuilding where we know she cannot get to us. Hedra, you will remain there at all times, unless I call for you. Note that I said *I*. If you see anyone but me, or hear anyone but me, beckoning to you, ignore them because that will be a trick."

Robyn remembered the vision of Simon from yesterday. "But surely she can mimic anyone she chooses."

"There are some things even she isn't capable of," Meliora said. "And one is mimicking another witch. She knows my powers as I know hers. If she were to manifest as me, her powers would fail and be passed onto me."

"What else shall we do, Meliora?" Hedra asked.

"You will do nothing. Your relationship to Chesten Denzel will not help us in there at this time. Merely watch and wait and never leave the sanctuary of the outbuilding. Not even for a second. If you do, you will put us all in danger, for she will use you to get at us."

"What do you want me to do?" Robyn asked, fearful of the reply.

"You and I will face her together. We must banish her from the cottage and send her back to hell."

"When you say it like that, you make it sound so straightforward."

"It will be anything but that, I'm afraid. You are already aware of how devious she can be and all you had was a taste of that yesterday. You must stay close to me at any cost. Don't believe her lies. Believe only what I tell you. Understand?"

"Yes."

Hedra pulled up behind the cottage. Once again, there was no sign of the crow. Maybe it was too preoccupied with terrifying an innocent young girl in London.

The three women climbed out of the car. Meliora raised her hands skyward and muttered an incantation. She shook herself and pointed at the outbuilding.

Robyn unlocked the door. The women stepped over the threshold. As before, the comforting smell of the logs greeted them.

Meliora handed Robyn a tightly bound bunch of asafetida. The stench of rotten eggs and a sewage-like smell made her retch.

"It's not so bad when you burn it." Meliora extracted a box of matches from her pocket and lit the herb. The dung-like smell faded, replaced by an aroma of frying onions laced with garlic. Meliora lit her own bunch and hooked her basket over her arm. "We are ready. Come with me, Robyn."

Robyn followed a few paces behind, aware that Hedra watched them from inside the doorway of the outbuilding. After unlocking the back door to the cottage, Robyn mimicked Meliora's action in hoisting the smoking asafetida bunch in front of her. Inside, the stench of decay met them. The formerly bright kitchen seemed cloaked in darkness and there was a strange sound, a murmuring.

Meliora touched Robyn's arm and whispered, "She is here. She wanders. Upstairs, I think, in the girl's room. That's where her essence will be strongest in this house."

She beckoned Robyn to follow. Robyn forced her unwilling feet forward and up the stairs close behind Meliora.

At the top, Meliora reached in her basket and pressed a handful of seeds in Robyn's hand. "Sprinkle these behind you as you walk."

Robyn nodded. She did as instructed. At the door of each room, Meliora stopped and sprinkled a line of seeds along the threshold. She saved Petra's room for last. When she didn't move to sprinkle any seeds there, Robyn raised her hand, ready to do so.

Meliora stopped her and shook her head. "We want her to come out here. She will go no further. The seeds will stop her, but we want her out of that room. Once she is out here, we can seal it."

A heavy pall hung over the young girl's room turning the girly colors dingy and tawdry, dirty and gray. The stench was worse than the raw asafetida. Robyn put her free hand over her nose, breathing through her mouth. It didn't help much. She could taste the stench now.

She followed Meliora into the room, her heart beating wildly and noisily in her ears, while her skin crawled and her mind screamed at her to get out of there. Hardly daring to breathe, Robyn stood her ground, almost touching the white witch. Meliora stood silently, waiting. No one else accompanied them. No one Robyn could see at any rate, but she knew instinctively that they were being watched.

Some minutes went by until Meliora spoke to Robyn, thrusting the basket out toward her as she did so. "Take the two bunches of fumitory out, one at a time, and light them for me. Give one to me and hold onto the other."

Robyn had never seen fumitory before, but she deduced they must be the bunches of dried pink and red flowers. The remaining bunches were distinctive by both their musty smell and blueish-green leaves, rue. She did as Meliora instructed, relieved to find the fumitory gave off no noxious odors, merely a smoky, earthy odor.

Armed with two bunches of smoking herbs, Robyn followed close behind Meliora as she moved farther into the room.

An acrid stench clung to Robyn's nostrils—the combined effects of the herbs and the increasing shroud of decay that weighed down the room.

Meliora motioned for her to stand still. She handed her the basket while she circumnavigated the room, wafting the asafetida and fumitory.

Robyn felt something behind her. Heavy hands pressed down on her shoulders, forcing her to her knees.

She cried out to Meliora who spun round and pointed. "I see you now, daughter of Malan. Come out and face me."

Robyn struggled to stand but the force oppressing her proved too great to resist. "Meliora?"

"Hush, child. Stay calm."

Robyn concentrated on breathing, forcing her breath in and out, swallowing down the screams of panic that threatened to erupt inside of her.

Meliora's voice remained strong and clear. "Daughter of Malan. I command you, by the spirits of earth, air, fire, and water. Leave this place."

The raucous voice sounded from behind her right ear. "You command no one. Get thee away from my home. You have no business here."

"Let the girl go."

"She stays."

"Not while there is breath in my body."

"So shall it be."

The force dragged Robyn off the floor. It flung her across the room. She hit the chest of drawers, scattering Petra's unicorns and dolls, and landed in an agonizing heap on the floor. Pain shot through her arm and ankle, the basket's contents scattered everywhere. Smoking herbs licked the hems of the curtains. Any second and they would set them alight. Already they were smoking. She had to get there, stop them from burning, and retrieve the herbs.

Robyn crawled. Every movement sent fresh agony coursing through her body. She must get there. She couldn't fail.

A fierce wind whistled through the room. Robyn found she couldn't move. Something was paralyzing her. The gale swirled into a vortex. At its heart, shadowy figures battled each other. Some shimmered with gold and silver auras. Others were shrouded in black and charcoal. Although the wind didn't reach her, the stench of sulfur it gave off was so strong, it made her retch.

Across the room, Meliora seemed to grow taller. Her eyes glittered. She stretched out her arms toward the vortex, bellowing over the raging, scirocco-like howl. She chanted an incantation in some unfamiliar language. With one almighty gust, the figures within the whirlwind twisted together, spinning faster and faster, as if inextricably entwined.

In a flash of brilliant light, they were gone. The room was deathly quiet.

Robyn flexed her fingers. The paralysis seemed to have gone as fast as it had come on. She tried to stand, but her ankle buckled and she sank back down onto the floor. Horrified, she watched Meliora fall forward. The old woman let out one sigh and went still.

"*No*," Robyn cried. She must get to Meliora. But there was an even more pressing problem.

The curtains. The smell of singeing fabric had overtaken that of the sulfur. One last herculean effort brought Robyn within a fingertip reach of the smoking herbs. She grabbed them, and a faint wisp of smoke died away from the curtains. A couple of more seconds and they would have been alight. Robyn stubbed the herbs out against the wall, leaving filthy marks there, but at least they could do no more immediate damage.

Job done, Robyn crawled toward Meliora, whose body lay inert. If only she would show some sign of life, but she didn't move. Robyn clasped the woman's wrist, feeling for a pulse and failing to find one. Then, a few feet away, a shape formed. At first hunched. it grew by the second.

Jowanet stood before her, fully manifested but different than before. Younger, and free of the hideous black quills. Her eyes were not flaming red, but black. Hypnotic. They held Robyn captive in their gaze.

The witch moved closer although Robyn never saw her take one step. She towered above her, and pointed a long, slender finger, its talon-like nail seeming to grow before her eyes. "You will bring my sister to me."

Robyn swallowed. "Never!"

The witch's lips moved back off her teeth in a hissing, hideous grimace. She curled her fist, then splayed her fingers. In the palm of her hand, a ball of swirling white light and black shadows twirled and spun faster and faster. Like Meliora earlier, Jowanet murmured some incantation in a language Robyn couldn't understand.

Her eyes would not stay open. She blinked, but the effort drained her too much. Slowly she drifted; eyes firmly shut, feeling as if she was floating. Without warning, a chill froze her skin and penetrated deep within her bones.

Her eyes sprang open. She was lying on a black ledge. It felt cold, wet and slimy against her body. No sign of Meliora, or Petra's room, nor even Malan Cottage. Panic welled up inside Robyn as she gazed about. She still wore her jeans and tee shirt and had sandals on her feet, but she was filthy. A sour smell emanated from her unwashed body. How long had she been here? More importantly, where the hell was she and how could she get out?

Instinctively, she reached for the hag stones around her neck. They weren't there. She must have dropped them somewhere. Or maybe someone, or something, had taken them. She must find them.

A shuffling sound came from behind her. Robyn turned.

A hideous figure, more than seven feet tall, rose up, its body covered in scales, head grotesque, and eyes blazing with unnatural fire. It opened its mouth and let out an earsplitting roar.

Robyn's consciousness slid deep. The demon's roar faded as a blanket of the densest black reached out to envelop her. She could see nothing, but, somewhere in here, she sensed Meliora's presence and with her, another protecting spirit.

If only she could find them.

CHAPTER FIVE

Holly looked around her. "What a mess."

Will pushed back his floppy fringe from his eyes. He picked up one of his daughter's dolls, its face twisted and blackened. "It looks like a battle royal took place here. Good thing Petra's not here to see this."

Holly nodded, then dropped the black bin liner she was holding and sank down onto Petra's bed. "Oh God, Will, where is she? Where's my sister? This isn't like her."

Will sat beside her, and, she leaned her head on his shoulder. He stroked her hair. "You read the letter," he said. "And you heard what Hedra said when we arrived. The whole mix of what's been happening here and the grief over Simon pushed her over the edge. Robyn felt she had to get away. She'll be back. I'm sure of that."

"But to go without telling us… After what had happened."

"She couldn't tell us, could she? We had no phone or internet contact."

"Then why didn't *she* write us the letter? Why leave it to a stranger?"

Will sighed. "We've been over that. Robyn and Hedra had grown quite close. Your sister regarded her as a friend, and, I can see why. Hedra seems to have taken her under her wing. *She* doesn't seem worried, and, she was the last person to see her before she took off."

"The police aren't doing anything."

"I told you they wouldn't. You did your bit by reporting her as a missing person, but, to them, she isn't. She's an adult with no record of mental illness who, by her own volition, decided to go away for a rest. They have no reason to suspect foul play."

"She left her car. It's still outside."

"Hedra told you she drove Robyn to the train station. Your sister didn't feel up to driving. Quite understandable, given the circumstances."

"But Hedra has no idea where she went, and, I don't understand why she didn't see her onto the train."

"She told you. Robyn wanted to be by herself, incognito."

Holly wiped the tear that was tracking its way down her cheek. She sat up and looked around her. "We can't keep this place. Not after all that's happened."

"The way things are, we stand to lose a packet if we sell now."

Holly turned on her husband. "Are you honestly suggesting we bring Petra and Xander here after what's happened? We daren't even bring our daughter back to her own home at the moment, and, I'm running out of excuses to tell—"

Will raised a warning hand. "Don't mention the name. Remember where we are and who might be listening."

Holly stood and yelled at the top of her voice. "You filthy bitch. Why can't you leave us alone? Go back to Hell where you belong."

A rush of fetid air swirled around the room, nearly knocking Holly off her feet.

Will grabbed her arm and steered her toward the door. "Let's get the hell out of here."

They ran down the stairs but as her foot hit the bottom step, Holly caught sight of the window ledge above the front door and pointed. "Look. There's something sticking out there. Right by the vase. I didn't put it there."

Will followed her gaze. "I'll get the steps." He dashed off to the utility room and was back within seconds. He set up the step stool and climbed it. "It's the other doll-thing." He reached up as if to remove it.

"Don't. Leave it there. Robyn said she had put it somewhere where it might do some good, and, we need all the help we can get."

Will nodded and climbed down. "I feel like this place is crowding in on me," he said. "I need some fresh air. Come on. Maybe a walk will clear our heads."

White clouds drifted lazily across the clear blue sky, as seabirds glided and danced, calling out, some diving into the sparkling water. Late afternoon on a perfect summer day. The contrast with her own feelings was almost too much for Holly. She and Will walked for an hour along the cliff top, mostly in silence, each wrapped in their own thoughts. They came across a bench and sat, looking out to sea.

Will broke the silence. "Did you see the old woman who scurried out of the café when we arrived this afternoon?"

"Yes. Lots of white hair. Looked doddery but moved like someone half her age."

"That's the one. I immediately thought of Meliora, that white witch Robyn mentioned, so when you went to the Ladies' I asked Hedra about her. She responded in an odd way."

"Odd? How?"

"It didn't really occur to me at the time. In fact, it's only now that I realize her reaction wasn't quite right. I mean, you would expect when someone says, 'Oh, was that the white witch, Meliora?' you would get a response such as, 'That's right' or 'No, that was…whoever' or even a simple, if unhelpful, 'No.' "

"So how did she respond?"

"She didn't reply. Made up some story about leaving the grill on, which was a bit odd, as we were the only ones in the café. There was no smell of anything grilling, and we had only ordered coffees. She then bolted into the back, and that was that. I still have no idea whether we saw Meliora…and another thing."

"Yes?"

"Why did the woman leave in such a hurry?"

"Maybe she was late for an appointment."

"Possibly. Somehow, I don't think so." Will stood, looked over at the horizon, and then turned back to Holly. "It never occurred to me before but maybe you're right to be suspicious about Hedra's version of events. I think someone around here's hiding something."

Holly put her head in her hands, overwhelmed by the implication of what Will had said. "I don't know what to wish for now. If you're right and someone knows more about Robyn's disappearance than they're letting on, that adds a whole new dimension to this. Will, I'm so scared. What do we do now?"

"Tomorrow, the glazier's coming, right?"

"Yes. I still don't know what happened to that window."

"That's not important. He can get on with his work, and we can leave him to it while we go into St. Oswell and track down Meliora. I have a feeling she has the answers."

"We should have done that straightaway when we got here." Holly looked at her watch. "It's after five. The shops will be shut by the time we get there." The breeze turned suddenly chilly and Holly shivered. "Let's go back home."

"Good idea."

They hurried back. Holly guessed Will was filled with as much trepidation as she was. Where was Robyn and what had really happened to her? Holly offered up a silent prayer and wondered if her husband was doing the same thing.

They were soon back at the cottage. As they arrived, a large black crow landed on the roof of the outbuilding and let out a loud *caw*.

Holly remembered what Robyn had told her, shivered again, and locked the back door behind them.

The following morning the workman duly arrived, a little after eight-thirty. Holly and Will sorted him out, telling him where the tea and coffee were and leaving Will's number should he need to contact them.

"We shouldn't be too long. Got a few errands to run," Holly said, careful to keep her voice light. "If you finish before we get back, just make sure the window and door are locked before you leave."

The glazier acknowledged them with a wave, and the couple set off for St. Oswell. Will drove.

"I don't think we should go into the tearooms," he said. "If I'm right, Hedra won't tell us the truth about Meliora anyway. We're best off trying to find her by other means. One of the other shops. Or the church even."

"Yes, but in a tight little community like that, everyone knows everyone else. They'll probably clam up with strangers."

Will cast Holly a quick glance before resuming concentration on the winding road ahead. "I hear what you're saying but have you got any better ideas?"

"No. But I don't think we should get our hopes up."

"Oh, believe me, mine aren't anywhere above floor level."

"Mine neither."

They parked on High Street outside the butcher's and got out of the car. "Let's try here." Will strode forward, but Holly grabbed his arm. "Look at the shop sign."

" 'R. and S. Trescothick Family Butchers'. So, what's wrong with that?"

Holly nodded across the street at Hedra's Tea Rooms. Underneath the sign…

" 'Hedra Trescothick,' " he read. "See what you mean. That's going to be a problem around here as well. Everyone not only knows each other, but they're probably related as well."

"Let's try the church. It's only up the hill. Maybe one of the worthy ladies of the parish is cleaning or doing the flowers for Sunday."

The sound of a mower grew louder as they approached the ancient building. An elderly man, wearing a baseball cap that looked as if his grandson might have loaned it to him, was engaged in mowing the grass along neat rows of gravestones. He did not register their presence until they were almost up to him. When he did, he gave a startled jump and killed the engine.

Holly pasted on a smile. "Good morning."

The man removed his cap and ran a clean white handkerchief over his face. "'Morning. Can I do something for you?"

He seemed wary but that was probably because he didn't know who they were. Holly felt gratified that at least he didn't appear hostile.

"We're looking for a lady called Meliora. I wondered if you could point us in the right direction."

"And you would be?"

"Oh, sorry. I'm Holly Prescott, and this is my husband, Will."

She stuck out her hand. He removed the gardening glove on his right hand and shook each of theirs in turn. "Robert Trescothick".

Holly's hopes vanished. "Any relation to the lady from the tea rooms?"

"I'm her father. My son and I are the local butchers. It's my day off today, so I'm helping out the vicar while the usual gardener's in hospital with a broken leg. Now, what do you want with Meliora? She a friend of yours? Doubt it, though."

"No, well not directly." Holly wished she had lied. Now he'd never tell them.

He studied her, his head slightly cocked. "You look familiar. Have you been around here long?"

Will spoke up. "We bought the cottage at Malan."

Holly wanted to throttle him.

Robert Trescothick's expression didn't change. "I've seen another young woman. Looks a lot like you, Mrs. Prescott."

"When did you last see her?"

"Not for a few days now. You'll be her sister, am I right? Hedra told me she'd been in touch when the girl went away."

No point in denying it. "That's right. Robyn, my sister, mentioned she'd received a lot of help from an older lady called Meliora. I believe she's a…" Remembering where she was, she stopped herself from saying those words. White witch. Hardly appropriate for a church graveyard.

Mr. Trescothick finished her sentence. "A witch. Oh, she's that all right. And more. I doubt she would have been much help to your sister, though. Evil, that woman is, make no mistake about it."

His words hit Holly like a stone. "But I understood her to be a friend of your daughter? A sort of…white witch…a wise woman, I think they used to call them."

Robert Trescothick gave a light laugh. "*White* witch? Meliora Penrose? Lord preserve us. She's descended from some of the *blackest* witches you could ever have the misfortune to come across. You should know something of them. They used to live in a house that stood right where your cottage is today. Meliora Penrose has always sworn she'll never rest until she gets back her heritage and restores the Malan witches to their rightful home. She'll stop at nothing, you know. You'd do well to keep away from her. Far away. Don't go courting evil, or it'll find you right enough, with no help whatsoever."

Holly mentally reeled from the impact of his words.

Will, meanwhile, found his voice. "I believe I saw her in your daughter's tea rooms yesterday. She ran out when we came in."

"Aye, she would. I don't doubt she was in there. My daughter has been doing all she can to get out of her clutches, but Meliora is a powerful, malevolent presence. If you want my advice, I'd get out of Malan and never return. Let her have her cottage back. Maybe then she'll leave the rest of us alone."

The starting up of the mower engine signaled the end of the conversation. Holly and Will were left watching Robert Trescothick, as he resumed his work. Will tapped Holly on the shoulder, and nodded toward the street. She followed him out of the graveyard.

"What do you make of that?" Will asked.

Holly felt bewildered. "I don't know who to believe. I mean, what we've been hearing is so different to Robyn's take on it. She believed Meliora to be a good witch, and now we're expected to believe the exact opposite."

"We've got to find this Meliora and have it out with her, or at least be able to make up our own minds."

"Agreed. But what do we do? Knock on every door?"

"If that's what it takes, why not? It's only a small village."

They were making their way down High Street. Holly stopped outside a florist. Buckets filled with an assortment of roses in every color imaginable, along with chrysanthemums, dahlias, and other flowers she didn't know the names of, adorned the shop front.

"Let's try here," she said. "Who knows? We may strike lucky and find someone who isn't related to the Trescothicks."

She pushed open the door and a heady mix of scented flowers and leaves, tinged with compost, greeted them. A young woman Holly gauged to be around her own age, or maybe younger, was arranging the makings of a stunning bouquet. She looked up at them and smiled.

"Good morning."

"Good morning," Holly replied. "I wonder if you can help us. We're looking for a woman called Meliora Penrose."

The smile disappeared. "I'm sorry, I can't help you." The woman returned to her task.

Holly and Will exchanged glances.

It was Will's turn. "Look, I'm sorry if we've hit a nerve or something, but we really need to talk to her. We're Will and Holly Prescott. We own Malan Cottage, and, my sister-in-law—Holly's sister that is—disappeared a few days ago. We're anxious to trace her."

The woman looked up again. "I heard about it. I'm sorry, but I really can't help you. I have no idea where she went. I understand she wanted some privacy, following a bereavement. That's all I know. Now, please, if you haven't come in to buy anything, I'm really busy today."

Will slapped his hand on the shop counter, and the woman jumped. "What is it about that woman, Meliora Penrose? And what is the problem with everyone in this bloody village? My sister-in-law is missing, and unless we find out what happened, and find out damned soon—"

"Who wants to see me so badly?"

At the sight of the newcomer, the shopkeeper shrank behind her counter. Holly recognized the woman in the doorway as the same one she had seen leaving Hedra's tea rooms. "You must be Meliora Penrose."

"And you are?"

Will extended his hand. "Holly and Will Prescott. Pleased to meet you."

Meliora looked him up and down but made no move to shake his hand. Will lowered it.

The woman addressed the shopkeeper. "It's all right, Karen. Have no fear. I only came in because I saw these two here. I shan't be staying." She motioned to Will and Holly. "You two had better come with me."

They followed her out of the florist's. Holly noticed a woman carrying a shopping bag crossed herself and hurried to the opposite side of the street to avoid passing them. Whatever, or whoever, Meliora Prescott was, she certainly had the power to instill fear in her neighbors. Could this really be the helpful white witch Robyn had told them about?

The woman faced them, her face expressionless. Holly was struck by the intensity of her gaze. Almost hypnotic.

"I know why you're here. I've been expecting you." Her expression clouded, and she frowned. "I hope you haven't brought the children."

"No," Holly said. "They're staying with friends."

The woman nodded. "The work we have to do is no place for them."

"Work?" Will asked.

"You want me to get her back for you, don't you?"

Holly's heart leaped. "You know where she is?"

"Of course."

"Then let's go and get her. Now."

"Not so fast. You can't really believe it would be that easy, can you? Your sister isn't simply staying in a house down the road. She isn't even in this world. No, Robyn is in a dark place. To return her will not be easy. Take me to Malan Cottage now, and I will start the work. I will need you, Holly. Will, I don't need you as you are not a blood relative. It is better that you not remain in the cottage while we do what is necessary. The witch may decide to use you, and, that is the last thing we need."

Holly looked at Will, and he nodded. They made their way to the car and Meliora climbed into the back. "Holly, switch off your phone and give it to Will. There must be no negative or artificial energies to drain my power. Once we arrive at the cottage, you must switch off all the electricity. We will then need at least half an hour before I can commence. You will do as I say, without question, at all times. Is that understood?"

They replied in unison. "Yes."

"We've heard some weird things about you, Meliora," Holly said. "From people in the village."

"Robert Trescothick, no doubt. He has it in his head that his daughter is under a spell of mine. That I have bewitched her in some way. He carries the hatred of his ancestors for my kind, but his daughter is more enlightened."

"He seemed quite adamant, and then the woman in the florist shop…"

Meliora made a scoffing noise. "Silly little Karen Priestley who only stopped believing in unicorns when she turned eighteen. She looks up to Robert Trescothick. He's her uncle you see. Same blood."

"You were helping Robyn that day…when she disappeared, weren't you?"

"I was."

"What happened to her?" Holly couldn't keep the tremble out of her voice.

"We encountered the witch Jowanet and I fought with her. Your sister was stalwart, and, you should be proud of her strength and fortitude. Unfortunately, the witch caught me off guard and I lost consciousness. When I came to, Robyn was gone, and, the signs told me Jowanet had taken her to the Dark Place."

"Where is that?"

"Between worlds. That is all I can tell you. All I am permitted to tell you."

But Holly knew from her expression that it wasn't all. Not by any means. Meliora was keeping something from her. Something of vital importance. Holly stared at her, anxious not to miss one detail of their encounter.

"Have the police been to see you?" Will asked.

"They have not." Meliora's response was tinged with indignation. "The local constabulary know me. I have known both of them since before they were born."

"And that's why the police haven't questioned you at all?"

"They know better. If I had anything to tell them, they know I would do so without waiting for them to come to me."

In this day and age? Such a contrast with London, but then, St. Oswell was a remote backwater. It didn't feature on anyone's radar. That's why they had bought a home here. Right now, Holly had an overwhelming desire to sell the place as quickly as possible. All its charm, the rugged and majestic coastline, and the peace and tranquility of nature all around them, far from the claustrophobic atmosphere of the big city, had turned toxic.

Holly shuddered. "How will you do it?" she asked. "Get Robyn back, I mean."

"I cannot promise anything. A lot will depend on the manifestation Jowanet chooses. Remember, we not only have to try to get your sister back. We also have to rid the cottage of the malicious spirit you unleashed."

That smarted. Holly opened her mouth to say something, caught Will looking at her out of the corner of his eye, and shut it again. It wouldn't do any good to antagonize Meliora. Besides, essentially, she was right. Holly would have to live with that knowledge for the rest of her life.

At the cottage, Meliora got out of the car first. The glazier's van was still there. Will turned to Holly. "Are you sure about this?"

"We have to try. It could be our last chance to get Robyn back. We can't afford to hang around."

"I don't like leaving you."

"You don't have to go far. Just keep out of sight for an hour or so."

"I'm still not happy—"

Holly kissed him. "I'll be fine. She's not the evil witch some people would have us believe. I'm convinced of that." And if she kept telling herself that, maybe she *would* actually believe it.

She waved Will off and put the key in the back door. Without warning, the door was dragged out of her hand. The glazier, his face white and eyes blazing, pushed past her.

"What the—?"

"I'm sorry, Missus. I can't finish the job. There's...there's something in there." He caught sight of Meliora. "Oh my God, what the fuck is *she* doing here?"

Meliora took a step forward and the man took off. He dragged open the door of his van.

"Don't go in there. For the love of God... And get away from *her*." He gunned the engine. The tires skidded as he slammed his foot down hard on the gas pedal.

Holly stared in disbelief as a cloud of sand and exhaust followed the terrified man.

Meliora put a calming hand on her arm. A gentle gesture, but, where her hand had lain, even so briefly, Holly's skin felt ice-cold.

"It looks like Jowanet arrived here early." Meliora gave a slight smile. "Come, Holly, we have work to do."

Holly swallowed hard and forced herself to concentrate on the matters in hand. First the electricity must be switched off. She understood Meliora couldn't help her. She must not touch anything in that cottage for at least half an hour.

From the open doorway, Meliora pointed at the windowsill. "How long have *they* been there?"

Holly looked to where she had indicated. Two large smooth pebbles she couldn't remember seeing before lay side by side, a thin piece of red cord threaded through identical holes in the center of each one. She picked them up, noting how freezing cold they felt against her skin. "I have no idea. Maybe Robyn found them on the beach. Someone's made a necklace out of them." She didn't say how she wouldn't have been caught wearing something like that. From the look of Meliora's eccentric attire, they would probably be just her style.

The old woman sighed. "Bring them to me. Put them on the ground by my feet. I can touch nothing that is in the cottage yet."

Holly did as requested. Then she switched off the electricity.

Meliora picked up the stones and clasped them tight, one in each palm. "I am sorry, but you are going to have to go upstairs and check that everything is as it should be. All windows must be tightly closed, in all the rooms."

Holly's throat closed up. She dreaded going up there. It had been bad enough with Will beside her, but on her own…

Meliora gave her a slight smile. "Do it now, while you have the courage."

Holly nodded and made herself run up the stairs. She left Petra's room until last. Once in there, Holly bit her lip and forced herself to ignore the awful mess while she concentrated on her immediate reason for being there. The window. She struggled over the debris, cringing with every step, until she reached it. It was shut fast.

She was back at the door, about to leave, when she heard a loud *caw*, coming from that same window.

She turned back to see a large crow land on the sill. It stared at her, and, she knew it was the same one she had seen before. The same one Robyn must have encountered. She shuddered and left the room.

"Did you see anything up there?" Meliora asked as Holly, her heart still racing, stepped outside to join her. She pointed up at the bird still perched on Petra's windowsill.

Meliora looked up. "Ah yes. One of her many manifestations. Come, we will wait in the outbuilding until it is time to begin."

Was it Holly's imagination? The pounding waves seemed louder this afternoon. She unlocked the door and they entered, the sweet smell of applewood greeting them.

"We have already established that this is a safe place. A mummified cat was placed here many years ago. The crow cannot enter."

"I didn't know about the cat—"

"It was well hidden and is so again. Come, sit with me. I must prepare, so we must stay in perfect silence until I say it is time to go."

"I understand." Holly listened to the waves, the call of the seagulls. A scrabbling on the roof and a raucous cry announced the arrival of the crow. It was reassuring to know it couldn't get in, but the sound of its claws tapping along the aged roof slates seemed unnaturally loud. Maybe her senses were heightened by this whole experience.

Meliora's eyes remained closed as time ticked by.

It seemed an age before Meliora opened her eyes. She stood up from the box she had been sitting on. "It is time. Let us go."

Holly nodded and tried to moisten her lips, but her mouth was too dry. Without a word, she followed Meliora outside. Holly noted the woman was still fingering the pebble necklace, turning it over and over, the stones making a soft clicking noise.

"Do they mean anything?" she asked.

"Yes. These are hag stones. Powerful witch's magic designed for a number of purposes, depending on the need at the time. The last time I saw these, they were around Robyn's neck."

"*What?*" Robyn's taste in jewelry had been understated. A simple gold chain, plain ring. Even her wedding band had been plain yellow gold, no adornment whatsoever.

Meliora's lips twisted in a slight grin which stopped at her mouth and faded instantly. "They were meant to afford her protection but, as I have said, we are dealing with a force so powerful, even two hag stones proved insufficient. I can only hope that, as these stones have found their way back here, so shall she. There is a force for good in there with her. She isn't alone."

"A force for good? What is it?"

Meliora shrugged and shook her head. "As yet, I have no idea. But be comforted by that. The fight is not over yet. Not by any means. Now. Invite me in. It is time to begin."

"Meliora, please come in."

The crow gave a loud squawk, further rattling Holly's already shredded nerves, and took off from the roof of the outbuilding. It soared high and out of sight.

Meliora crossed the threshold and immediately made her way up the stairs, Holly close behind her. The old woman paused at the door of Petra's room. "Are you ready? "

Holly was anything but ready, but she nodded.

Meliora gave her arm a squeeze. "Come, let us do our work." She lifted her ankle-length skirt and picked her way over the mess on the floor before taking up position in the center of the room and motioning Holly to stand next to her. Then Meliora muttered something under her breath Holly couldn't make out before lifting her hands high above her, fingers splayed. She called out, her voice strong and true.

"Jowanet, daughter of Malan, I command your presence and demand you bring the sister of the one who stands with me this day."

The air seemed to shift, become thicker, denser, but, as yet, there was no sign of the witch.

"Jowanet, daughter of Malan, I call on the spirits of earth, air, fire, and water to bring you into my presence."

The air grew opaque, as if night were descending at an accelerated rate. In the corner of the room, a dark shadow formed. As Holly watched, it undulated and swirled, taking on substance. Next to her, Meliora's breathing became raspy, labored... It seemed whatever had joined them was draining strength from her. But her voice remained firm.

"Jowanet, daughter of Malan, hear my words and do my bidding. Bring Robyn Crowe to me now."

The shadow settled itself into a hooded figure, all in black. In the distance, through the open window, Holly could hear a car engine. Surely Will wasn't coming back yet. It was too soon. Not what they had agreed upon.

The figure raised its head slowly. It stretched out a clawed hand, yellowed, decayed talons that almost touched her. A putrid smell of decay and rot overpowering everything.

"Holly. Get behind me. Now."

Holly did as told. Meliora moved forward inches. Holly flinched from the face the figure now revealed. Blackened skin erupted with the nubs of crow feathers. High, sharp cheekbones—barely more than skeletal—black eyes that never blinked. The bird-like claws for hands clenched and unclenched.

Outside, the car pulled up and the engine cut out.

"I command you to bring me Robyn Crowe," Meliora said, her voice strong despite her breathing difficulties.

"I am not yours to command, unnatural daughter." The witch raised her claw and made as if to strike Meliora, but her opponent had anticipated this. With strength Holly would not have believed the old woman possessed, she flung the witch back across the room.

Sprawled on the floor, Jowanet drew back thin lips over decayed and blackened teeth. Her gray, worm-like tongue lolled out of her mouth as she hissed, spitting at her adversary as she got to her feet.

A noise of someone running up the stairs. A face at the door.

"Hedra!" Holly exclaimed.

Hedra looked from Holly to Meliora and then at Jowanet, who addressed her. "Bring me my sister's poppet," she said.

Hedra nodded and ran back down the stairs, returning a moment later with the doll.

"No," Holly cried. "You can't give it to her."

"She won't," said Meliora. "Because she is going to give it to me."

Holly watched, unable to do anything to prevent whatever was about to take place.

Hedra hesitated, looking from one witch to the other, as if trying to make up her mind.

"Hedra, please…" Holly put her hand out, forgetting her former revulsion for the thing in the woman's hand. If only Hedra would give *her* the doll.

Jowanet pointed at the poppet "Remove the bodkin."

"No!" Holly tried to move forward but found she couldn't. Something was paralyzing her. She struggled. The force tightened its grip until every muscle and sinew in her body ached with the effort of resisting it.

Hedra carried on shifting her gaze from one to another.

Jowanet spoke again, her voice echoing from the depths of hell itself. "You will remove the bodkin. My sister shall be released."

Meliora began to glow. An aura of white light shone around her, rendering her almost angelic, but her power came from another source. On the far side of the room, in the opposite corner to the Malan witch, another shape formed—and Holly hardly dared believe.

"Robyn."

Her sister seemed trapped behind a force-field. Unconscious, asleep or…Holly didn't want to imagine that other possibility. A figure, in shimmering white, stood behind her, arms around her, but not imprisoning her. Protecting her. Caressing her.

Simon.

Jowanet lunged for the poppet but couldn't grasp it.

Meliora spoke. "You know even *your* power isn't great enough to break the spell Chesten Denzel wove into it. Be gone from this place and leave Robyn Crowe here, among the living, where she belongs."

"There is a price to be paid, and I claim it." She pointed at Holly. "My sister for her sister."

Holly held her breath. Hedra still held the doll.

Meliora addressed the witch, Jowanet. "Daughter of Malan, you bewitched this female, Hedra Trescothick, to do your will. You caused her to befriend the woman Robyn Crowe, to win her trust, but you reckoned without me."

Jowanet hissed again. "I do not fear you, though you be not as others see you."

"Alive, you were the stronger, but now we meet as equals. Now I am as you."

Holly stopped mid-breath, tearing her gaze away from the impossible vision in front of her. "Meliora, what are you saying?"

Meliora continued to focus all her attention on Jowanet. The contrast between them could not have been greater. The decayed hag with her stench of death, and the glowing white witch who seemed to be growing stronger; her power increasing with every second. With it, the semi-transparent force-field around Robyn grew clearer, as if Meliora was drawing her power directly from it. Robyn stirred slightly but did not open her eyes. Simon's aura faded to little more than a faint glow. Then blinked out altogether.

Holly let out her breath.

Meliora spoke again. "I have the power to release Hedra from your control, and I do so now."

Hedra dropped the doll and raced out of the room.

Meliora pointed at Jowanet. "Be gone from this place. You leave without your sister. It is finished."

Outside, Hedra's car revved and sped off, momentarily distracting Holly.

The Malan witch screamed as a horde of claw-like hands and grotesque bodies rose up to envelop her, claiming her as their own. Holly watched, mesmerized. In a brilliant flash of light, Jowanet and her assailants were gone, leaving the faintest echo of her screams and the cries of souls in torment.

"Holly? What happened?"

Robyn stood in front of her, dazed and filthy. Holly didn't care. She threw her arms around her, hugging her bemused sister, raining kisses and tears on her. "Oh Robyn, thank God you're back. Meliora did it, she…" Her voice tailed off as she realized they were alone. Meliora had vanished too. From her demeanor, it seemed Robyn had little—if any—recollection of what had happened to her.

The next day, despite their searches, Holly, Robyn, and Will could find no trace of the poppet.

"I know where Hedra dropped it," Holly said. "I saw her do it. But I never saw it after that."

"I have an idea," Will said. "I think Meliora either sent it to Hell with Jowanet or somehow spirited it back to its rightful hiding place somewhere in the chimney."

Robyn nodded. "It makes sense, doesn't it? What will you do with Malan Cottage now?"

Holly and Will replied as one. "Sell it."

"It's either that or lease it out as a holiday rental," Holly added. "I know the witch has gone, but we can't live here after all this. It wouldn't feel right. I'd never feel fully safe again and, as for Petra…"

"There's another thing I won't miss about this place," Will said. "The lousy signal. When you do get one, it sounds like someone's frying eggs half the time. I think I even got a crossed line when I phoned work earlier. I thought that went out with rotary telephone dials."

They laughed and Robyn joined in. It felt good. She would have to learn to live with the gaps in her recent memory, or maybe it would come back one day. Perhaps it was as Holly said when she mentioned it to her, better if she didn't remember. Yet one memory refused to be so easily dismissed.

Simon.

He had been there, with her, in the Dark Place. He had touched her, held her. The demon Malan should have taken her. Could have taken her. But it had stopped short of that. She could never explain it, but instinctively she knew, Simon had somehow saved her—and he had sent her the hag stones. When they had not been enough to protect her, he had come himself. Who knew at what risk to his immortal soul? Robyn fingered the stone necklace, once again restored to her neck. It comforted her and made her feel a little closer to him. If she concentrated really hard, she could almost imagine the surface of the stones was the smooth skin she had stroked so many times in their years together.

Will clapped his hands. "Okay, you two. Now that the window's finally repaired and we've finished Petra's room—"

"What *used* to be Petra's room," Holly said.

"I stand corrected," Will said. "How about going to the pub and having a bar meal?"

"Not St. Oswell, if you don't mind," Holly said. "I've had a bellyful of the local people around here. You never know who you can trust."

"Oh, I don't think Hedra's a bad person." Robyn said. "It wasn't her fault. The witch got to her. Probably it was because of her family's involvement with the burning of the two witches. Jowanet's perverted need for revenge meant she used their descendant."

Holly sighed. "Nearly getting you killed as a result. And let's not forget Meliora. I suppose by her disappearance we have to assume the witch killed her. I feel so sad about that because, without her, we wouldn't have *you* back, Robyn." She gave her sister a big hug.

And, in that instant, Robyn was back there. The strange limbo she somehow knew was called the Dark Place. Malan Cottage. Her sister. Brother-in-law. All gone.

No, *she* was the one who had gone. *They* were where they should be.

"Robyn."

The distant female voice could only belong to one person. Meliora. She didn't have an accent as such. An intonation. Robyn couldn't remember noticing it before. As if English was not her first language, and yet she had lived in St. Oswell seemingly forever.

"Robyn."

The voice was right behind her this time. "Meliora?" Robyn peered into the darkness surrounding her. She could see no one.

"Take my hand."

"Where are you? I can't see you."

"I am right here."

Meliora's face seemed to manifest itself out of the blackness. Robyn was past asking questions. Nothing about this place made any sense. It couldn't exist, but it did.

"What happened to you?" Robyn's question was out before she could think about it.

"I have come back to where I belong."

"That witch. Jowanet. What did she do to you?"

"Nothing at all. She had no power over me."

"But I saw what happened, in Petra's room. You collapsed on the floor, and you weren't breathing."

"But I have never breathed. Not as you. I have been in your world for centuries, but I am not part of it."

"I don't understand."

"You understand more than you think. You have been to this place, and you have survived it. Not many of your kind can say that."

The memory of the creature Robyn had seen the last time she had been in the Dark Place surfaced in her mind.

"Malan," Meliora said. "You are remembering your encounter with the Devil's henchman."

Robyn nodded. "Is he here?"

"No. He has gone. For now, at least. But Robyn, I must warn you, and I do not have much time before I too must leave. You must be careful. Be especially watchful of Petra."

"I thought the witch was gone."

"From Malan Cottage, yes. But something is still free. It is searching, always searching."

"Then what should we do?"

"You must go down to the beach; you, Holly, and Will. Tomorrow morning just as the tide goes out and the fresh, wet sand is untainted. By Malan Cove you must search among the rocks and in the pools. You must find a hag stone. It has to be one you find there and then. You cannot use one of your own. It will not work. When you find it, cut some red cord from your necklace and make one for Petra. Make sure her mother places it around Petra's neck as soon as they are reunited. The child must never take it off. Not even for a second and not for the rest of her life. As long as she wears it, she is protected. Swear you will do this."

Robyn nodded. "I swear."

"It must be her mother who places it around her neck. That too is vital."

"I understand."

"Robyn! Wake up!"

Robyn opened her eyes to find the anxious eyes of her sister staring into her face. Holly lowered her arms from where they had been shaking her sister's shoulders.

"Oh, sorry. I must have dropped off." Robyn looked around. She was back in the cottage, sitting on the settee in the living room. Will was watching her, seeming to search for answers in her face.

"You had me worried there for a moment," Holly said. "One minute we were talking and the next you seemed to drift off into some kind of daze."

Robyn put her hand to her head. "I had a really weird dream about Meliora."

Holly sighed. "Only natural given the circumstances, I suppose."

"Come on then," Will said, his cheerfulness a little forced. "Let's find that pub. There's bound to be another around here somewhere, without going into St. Oswell."

Robyn stood. "Actually, do you mind if I pass? I'm feeling so tired. I'd like to go to bed. And tomorrow morning, can we get up early and go down to the beach? There's something we need to do as soon as the tide has gone out. Don't ask me what, but, please, can we do that?"

Holly and Will exchanged confused glances.

"Of course," Holly said, at last. "If you say it's important, then it must be. We'll just put a pizza in the oven, and all have an early night."

Emerging into the bright sunshine the next morning, Robyn, Will and Holly set out for Malan Cove. Robyn found herself glancing around, looking for the crow. Holly caught her and smiled.

"I've just done the same. Force of habit. So, why are you so anxious to go to the beach now?"

"You need to bear with me," Robyn said. "It's a superstition, but we need to find protection for Petra." She fingered the hag stone necklace around her neck. "Yesterday, when you said I seemed to drift off, I told you I had dreamed about Meliora. Well, in that dream—or whatever it was—she told me we need to search the rocks and pools for a hag stone for her. We mustn't fail. We need them to make her a necklace like mine."

"What are we waiting for?" Will said. "Let's find that stone and then we can get away from this place." He broke into a run.

Robyn and Holly hurried to catch up with him. Beneath them, the water shimmered. The track down to the cove was steep, narrow, sandy, and riddled with potholes. Fortunately, someone had erected a handrail made from tree branches. Robyn grasped it and it swayed a little, but it was better than hurtling full pelt.

The breeze blew kisses of air across Robyn's cheeks, soothing her still-troubled soul. Dream or reality, her encounter with Meliora the previous evening remained clear and sharp in her mind. However crazy, they must do as she had instructed, and they must be successful. Petra's life and soul depended upon it.

They reached the bottom and stood on firm, sea-drenched sand on a beach strewn with seaweed and stones. Robyn stared around in dismay. With all these pebbles, how would they find the hag stone before the tide turned?

"Okay," Will said. "Meliora told you we should search among the rock pools, didn't she? She specifically mentioned rock pools?"

"She said we must search among the rocks and the pools. There are so many. It could be anywhere."

Will bit his lip. "I vote we take her literally." He looked around, then pointed at the overhanging cliff face. "Let's start over there. We'll each take a section."

"It's as good a place as any," Robyn said. Holly nodded.

Sheltered by the overhanging rock, their voices echoed, turning the stones echoed, the waves seemed muffled and far away. Smells of seaweed and a more unpleasant stench of rotting fish turned her stomach as Robyn concentrated on systematically inspecting each stone for a distinctive circular hole. Tiny, almost transparent crabs scuttled away as she dislodged them from their perches.

A small pile grew next to her—a mini cairn of discarded pebbles. To either side of her, Will and Holly were building their own spoil heaps. As each pool was eliminated, they moved farther out, and the eerie echoing grew less and less pronounced.

After more than an hour, Robyn's back ached for a rest from the awkward bending. Kneeling was an impossibility with so many stones around, so she battled through the pain.

Suddenly, Holly gave a whoop and straightened up, brandishing a little white stone in her hand. Robyn could see the small hole from where she was. Dropping the handful of stones she held, she started toward her, only to see Holly put the hole to her eye.

"Don't!"

Her sister screamed and threw the stone away from her. Will caught it, and he and Robyn reached Holly at the same time. Will held her tight. Holly's face had turned ashen. "I saw…"

"What?" Will asked. "What did you see?

Holly wrenched herself out of Will's grasp and stared straight at Robyn. "You know, don't you?"

"Was it a demon?"

"I...I don't know. More of a feeling... I can't describe it."

Robyn hugged her. "Hedra told me never to look through the hole of a hag stone. They are portholes. You can see through into the other world. They hold powerful magic, and, it can all go badly wrong if you misuse it. We need this stone for Petra. Come on, we've got to go now and get it to her."

Holly exhaled. "A week ago, I wouldn't have believed a word of what you just said. But I believe you now. I'll give it to her."

"No, you must actually fasten it around her neck. And she must never take it off, not for an instant, not ever."

Holly nodded. Will's face had drained of color, but he copied his wife's gesture. "Let's get back, load up the car, and get the hell out of this godforsaken place."

Robyn nodded, fingering the car keys in her pocket and wishing her heart would stop beating quite so fast. "I'll follow on behind you."

At her best friend's house in London, Petra Prescott opened her eyes. Something had fallen on her. She felt around and her fingers touched something unfamiliar. She was too sleepy to wake up and see what it was. That would have to wait until later.

She drifted back off to sleep.

In her hand, the poppet settled and waited.

ACKNOWLEDGEMENTS

My heartfelt thanks, as always, to my good friend and fellow writer, Julia Kavan, who reads my early drafts, has an uncanny knack of spotting where I have slipped, tripped, and wandered off into the realms of the totally ridiculous. She makes me a much better writer. Thank you, Julia.

Huge thanks to Ken McKinley, Ken Cain, and all at Silver Shamrock. I love working with you and look forward to many more projects.

Massive thanks to the many writers who inspire me on a daily basis—to Ramsey Campbell from whom I have learned so much and whose books are a constant (horrific) delight, Adam Nevill, Stephen King, Joe Hill, Paul Tremblay, Susan Hill, Hunter Shea, Jonathan Janz, Glenn Rolfe, J.H. Moncrieff, Simon Bestwick, Priya Sharma, Cate Gardner, Russell James, Stuart West, Somer Canon… The list is growing. Great to know our favorite genre is in such safe hands.

And to you for reading *The Malan Witch*. If you weren't there to do that, there wouldn't be much point in doing what I do. Thank you. I look forward to going on many more journeys into the dark, scary and sinister with you.

ABOUT THE AUTHOR

Catherine Cavendish first started writing when someone thrust a pencil into her hand. Unfortunately, as she could neither read nor write properly at the time, none of her stories actually made much sense. However, as she grew up, they gradually began to take form and, at the tender age of nine or ten, she sold her dolls' house, and various other toys to buy her first typewriter. She hasn't stopped bashing away at the keys ever since, although her keyboard of choice now belongs to her laptop.

The need to earn a living led to a varied career in sales, advertising and career guidance but Cat is now the full-time author of a number of supernatural, ghostly, haunted house and Gothic horror novels and novellas, including *The Malan Witch, The Garden of Bewitchment, The Haunting of Henderson Close*, and the Nemesis of the Gods series. Her short story "Euphemia Christie" appeared in the Silver Shamrock *Midnight in the Graveyard* anthology and another short story of hers is due to appear in their new *Midnight in the Pentagram* anthology. A new novel – *In Darkness, Shadows Breathe* – is due out in early 2021. She lives in Southport, in the U.K. with her longsuffering husband and black cat and can be found at www.catherinecavendish.com as well as the usual social media.

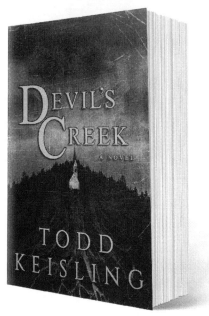

"Todd Keisling runs at the front of the pack."

—John Langan, Bram Stoker Award-winning author of *The Fisherman*

About fifteen miles west of Stauford, Kentucky lies Devil's Creek. According to local legend, there used to be a church out there, home to the Lord's Church of Holy Voices—a death cult where Jacob Masters preached the gospel of a nameless god.
And like most legends, there's truth buried among the roots and bones.

In 1983, the church burned to the ground following a mass suicide. Among the survivors were Jacob's six children and their grandparents, who banded together to defy their former minister. Dubbed the "Stauford Six," these children grew up amid scrutiny and ridicule, but their infamy has faded over the last thirty years. Now their ordeal is all but forgotten, and Jacob Masters is nothing more than a scary story told around campfires.

For Jack Tremly, one of the Six, memories of that fateful night have fueled a successful art career—and a lifetime of nightmares. When his grandmother Imogene dies, Jack returns to Stauford to settle her estate. What he finds waiting for him are secrets Imogene kept in his youth, secrets about his father and the church. Secrets that can no longer stay buried.

The roots of Jacob's buried god run deep, and within the heart of Devil's Creek, something is beginning to stir...

Manufactured by Amazon.ca
Bolton, ON